P9-CFK-088

DAPHNE DU MAURIER
Enchanted Cornwall

RENEWAL...
GENERAL LIBRARY

DUMECOR990

DAPHNE DU MAURIER
Enchanted Cornwall

HER PICTORIAL MEMOIR

Edited by
PIERS DUDGEON

Photographs by
NICK WRIGHT

VESTAVIA HILLS LIBRARY
Vestavia Hills, Alabama

MICHAEL JOSEPH · PILOT

MICHAEL JOSEPH LTD ·
PILOT PRODUCTIONS LTD

Published by the Penguin Group
27 Wrights Lane, London, W8 5TZ, England

in association with

Pilot Productions Limited
17 Munster Road, London, SW6 4ER

Viking Penguin Inc., 40 West 23rd Street,
    New York, New York 10010, USA
Penguin Books Australia Ltd, Ringwood, Victoria,
    Australia
Penguin Books Canada Ltd, 2801 John Street,
    Markham, Ontario, Canada L3R 1B4
Penguin Books (NZ) Ltd, 182-190 Wairau Road,
    Auckland 10, New Zealand

Penguin Books Ltd. Registered Offices,
Harmondsworth, Middlesex, England

First published September 1989
Second impression before publication

Copyright © Pilot Productions Limited, 1989
Text Copyright © Daphne du Maurier, 1989

All rights reserved. Without limiting the rights
under copyright reserved above, no part of this
publication may be reproduced, stored in or
introduced into a retrieval system, or transmitted, in
any form or by any means (electronic, mechanical,
photocopying, recording or otherwise), without the
prior written permission of both the copyright owner
and the above publisher of this book

Edited by Piers Dudgeon
Designed by Nigel Partridge
Typeset by Dorchester Typesetting, Dorchester,
    England
Printed by Printer Portuguesa, Mem Martins, Portugal

A CIP catalogue record for this book is available
from the British Library.
ISBN 0-7181-3326-9

Library of Congress Catalog Card Number
89-83914

CONTENTS

~

24.95 (14.97) ING 3-5-9

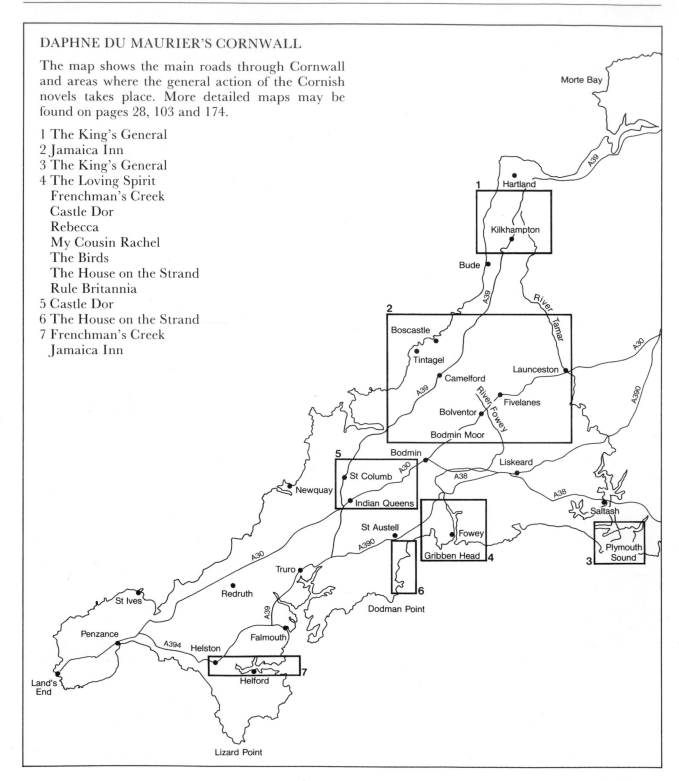

DAPHNE DU MAURIER'S CORNWALL

The map shows the main roads through Cornwall and areas where the general action of the Cornish novels takes place. More detailed maps may be found on pages 28, 103 and 174.

1 The King's General
2 Jamaica Inn
3 The King's General
4 The Loving Spirit
  Frenchman's Creek
  Castle Dor
  Rebecca
  My Cousin Rachel
  The Birds
  The House on the Strand
  Rule Britannia
5 Castle Dor
6 The House on the Strand
7 Frenchman's Creek
  Jamaica Inn

Morte Bay

1 Hartland

Kilkhampton

Bude

River Tamar

A39

A30

2 Boscastle

Tintagel

Camelford

Launceston

River Fowey

Fivelanes

Bolventor

A390

Bodmin Moor

Bodmin

Liskeard

A38

5 St Columb

A30

Indian Queens

A38

Newquay

St Austell

Saltash

Fowey

3 Plymouth Sound

A390

Gribben Head 4

6

Truro

Dodman Point

Redruth

St Ives

A39

Land's End

Penzance

A394 Helston

Falmouth

7

Helford

Lizard Point

FOREWORD

When this book was suggested my first instinct, invariably the same with any invitation, was to decline; I enjoy my solitude here at Kilmarth. People have told me that I am thought of as a recluse, which suggests someone who is very lonely, but there is a difference between loneliness and being solitary. The reason I am thought of as a recluse is that I don't go out socially. I don't go to dinners, lunches, or cocktail parties, and I don't wish to do the constant TV interviews which authors are now expected to give. But I'm not lonely, it's just that I've always liked being on my own. I suppose you could call me a loner.

I also recall being anxious in case the book turned out to be just another about the Cornish country-side. I was, however, attracted by the idea that it should be attached to my life as a writer. Certainly the places in my novels are generally places where I have been, but *Enchanted Cornwall* is more than a travelogue. It tries to give an idea of the way in which Cornwall has communicated with me, and I with Cornwall, for here I found myself both as a writer and as a person.

Cornwall became my text. Perhaps if it hadn't been Cornwall it would have been somewhere else, who knows? 'All England is a palimpsest,' wrote Sir Arthur Quiller Couch, the celebrated 'Q', in the prologue to our book, *Castle Dor* – a land, 'scored over with writ of hate and love, begettings of children beneath the hazels, betrayals, appeals, curses, concealed travails.'

I walked this land with a dreamer's freedom and with a waking man's perception – places, houses whispered to me their secrets and shared with me their sorrows and their joys. And in return I gave them something of myself, a few of my novels passing into the folk-lore of this ancient place.

In Cornwall I discovered especially a sense of timelessness barely glimpsed before. A sense of continuity with ancient times, and more than this, a present which resonated with past and future – a sense indeed that past, present and future are not isolated milestones in time, to be feared, longed for, and finally met, but that they are one, each part of a whole, existing side-by-side.

Likewise, in our beginning is our end. I who writes this, lives and dies, but something of myself goes into the children born of my body, and to their children, and those children's children. Life, what-ever shape or form it takes, goes on, is truly eternal.

My last book came out in 1981 and *Enchanted Cornwall* would not have been produced without the help of Piers Dudgeon, who has been more than an editor. He read all my works and sought out every nook and cranny where they are set. I shared my thoughts with him and he wove the threads into this pleasing tapestry.

Daphne du Maurier

CHAPTER ONE

IN THE WOOD OF THE WORLD

~

I was born on May 13th, 1907, into a world of make-believe and imagination. A year earlier my father, at the age of thirty-three, had enjoyed his first big acting success as Raffles, the suave cricketer turned cracksman who so delighted his Edwardian audiences.

Four years later he went into management with a non-acting partner, Frank Curzon, at London's famous Wyndham's Theatre in the Charing Cross Road, and for the next fifteen years, playgoers did not have to search the newspapers to discover where Gerald du Maurier was performing; it could only be at Wyndham's.

As a child I would sometimes go to fetch him from the theatre after a matinée performance. Thinking back, after all too many years, I can still feel the bars across the theatre swing doors under my hands; surely I had to reach up to them? And Bob, the stage doorkeeper, smiling down from his stool. The stairs to the dressing room, stage entrance on the left, stairs to the other dressing rooms on the right. The musty, indefinable smell of shifting scenery, with stage hands moving about and Poole, Daddy's dresser, who had rather a red face and mumbled as he spoke, hovering at the entrance to the dressing room.

To us children there was nothing singular or surprising that in a moment Daddy would come bursting in from the door that led direct backstage, calling for Poole, and that we would hear the distant sound of applause which meant that the audience was still clapping after the final curtain, before 'God Save the King'. This was his life. Other children's fathers, perhaps, went to an office; ours went to the theatre.

Often, friends or acquaintances who had been to the matinée would come round to see him, which meant standing up and shaking hands on our part, and listening, yawning, while the chatter passed over our heads. The people who came always seemed excited, thrilled; entering the star's dressing room was an

I was born into a world of make-believe and imagination.

Menabilly Woods. They had the magic quality of a place untrodden. Before I found them I was lost in the 'wood of the world'.
'I think that behind everybody's thoughts while he is growing there must be a forest.' Castle Dor

event. It was a relief when the exclamations and the congratulations were over and we were just ourselves, with Daddy sitting down and taking off his make-up at the dressing table. Pity, though, I sometimes thought. He looked nicer with it on, bolder, somehow, and his eyes very bright. Still, it was all part of the game of make-believe that was his, and ours as well.

Few of the plays that became such popular successes during Daddy's spell at Wyndham's would raise an eyebrow of recognition today. They were chiefly action packed, concerned with the thrill of the chase – *Raffles, Bulldog Drummond* – they were of their time – no doubt a mark of his management expertise in catching the mood of an era. It took James M Barrie to draw the finest acting out of the matinée idol of the day. In *Dear Brutus*, surely Barrie's best play, first performed in 1917, Daddy took the part of Will Dearth, a jaded, spoilt, successful painter, at odds with his wife and with the world. His transformation in the second act to the happy-go-lucky father – a dream sequence in an enchanted wood – saw Gerald du Maurier at his acting peak. He was himself, yes, but also every man who carries in his soul a seed of discontent, of wishing that his world was other than it had turned out to be. It was a performance which I, as a child of ten, would never forget.

By that time Barrie, fairy godfather to countless children, had become part of our family life. 1904 had seen the first performance

What a world of imagination we lived in then . . . my sister Angela, older than me by two years, was chosen by J M Barrie ('Uncle Jim' as we called him) to play Wendy to Gladys Cooper's Peter Pan.

*When I think of Gerald he had
pottered downstairs to the drawing
room one fine morning in search of
cigarettes, and he is wearing silk
pyjamas from Beale and Inman of
Bond Street, topped by a very old
cardigan full of holes that once
belonged to his mother. He switches
on the gramaphone, holds out his
arms to a non-existent partner and,
closing his eyes, circles the room with
the exaggerated rhythm of a musical-
comedy hero. Unseen, unobserved, so
he imagines, he obeys the instinct of a
lifetime and is acting to himself.*

of his abidingly famous children's play *Peter Pan*, about the boy
who never grew up. It had evolved from stories he had made up for
the five sons of his friends (my uncle and aunt) Arthur and Sylvia
Llewelyn Davies. Later, on Arthur and Sylvia's death, Barrie gave
the boys a home.

I remember once overhearing a conversation between the boys'
nanny and ours about cousin Michael: 'Michael has bad night-
mares. He dreams of ghosts coming through the window.' At night,
I would stare at the window of our nursery, and understand.

What a world of imagination we lived in then. *Peter Pan* – the
play that we went to see every Christmas, that we acted out
endlessly in our own nursery, once in front of the author himself.

Later my sister Angela, older than me by two years, was actually chosen by 'Uncle Jim', as we called him, to play Wendy to Gladys Cooper's Peter which caused great excitement. I didn't envy her. To appear before an audience on the stage would have been agony for me even in a play like *Peter Pan*, which both of us knew by heart.

I could see why Daddy liked to dress up and pretend to be someone else. *Life* was pretending to be someone else. Otherwise it was rather dull. But there was never a danger that I would follow Gerald into the profession. Instead I chose what, in hindsight, is probably just another form of acting.

Books became my life. I read tremendously from the age of four, and from the start I was always pretending to be someone else in a story. To begin with, there was Beatrix Potter; as soon as I could read properly her characters became my companions – Tom Kitten, Mrs Tiggy-Winkle, Peter Rabbit. There was the terrible rat with his rolling pin, angry Mr McGregor, sinister Mr Tod the fox. And Jeremy Fisher who made me shiver when he knocked,

My mother, Muriel Beaumont, met my father when they were acting together in Barrie's play, The Admirable Crichton *at the Duke of York's in 1902.*

leering, at Mrs Twitchet's door.

Sometimes as a treat, when Angela and I went downstairs to the drawing room for tea, Mummy would read to us aloud. I remember *The Snow Queen* in particular. The Queen was wicked. She drove through the snow in an icy chariot, taking a little boy with her, so that his blood would turn to icicles. His name was Kay. He had a little friend called Gerda, who finally rescued him. As I listened I became each child in turn, first Kay, then Gerda, and when Mummy had finished and it was time to go upstairs to bed, and Mummy pretended to chase us, it was not funny at all, I saw her as the Snow Queen and I was frightened.

Little books led to bigger books but they had to be exciting, they had to have adventures. They couldn't be fairy stories, they were silly. Tinkerbell was all very well in *Peter Pan*, but I knew the light that danced about on stage was really shone by one of the theatre men. They had to be stories with characters I could believe in, identify with, and act out with my sisters.

The Bible stories were good. But I liked Cain better than Abel, and Esau better than Jacob, and Joshua was a true hero, blowing his trumpet round the walls of Jericho. Best of all was David, slinging a stone at Goliath. Why wasn't I born a boy? They did all the brave things. Fought all the battles. As it was I had to make do with pretending, tuck my dress into my knickers, find a stick and wave it like a sword. Angela, on the other hand, did not mind being a girl. In our make-up games she'd take her part and throw open the window of the Wendy house in the garden calling, 'Save me, save me!' Then bravely I would slash at the bushes, our enemies,

It started with play, it started with being an imaginary person, and it's gone on that way ever since.

and run to her rescue.

Then, in 1915, I was given a copy of *Treasure Island* and from that moment a whole new world awaited me. I soon had the first page by heart. I was Jim Hawkins (with occasional lapses into Long John Silver). My younger sister Jeanne, who had been roped into our games almost as soon as she could walk, would come tapping along the garden path as Blind Pew while I crouched in an imaginary ditch, in the lane near the Admiral Benbow Inn. Jeanne understood little of her role, but this did not matter.

Other books followed – *The Wreck of the Grosvenor*: I was Edward Royle, the narrator, the young second mate, and if Jeanne could hardly bellow as the bully Captain Coxon at least she could shout, 'Clew up the main-sail and furl it,' and stamp her foot. 'The biscuits are full of weavils, the pork stinks,' I would mutter as we ate our lunch in the kitchen, and Jeanne nodded vigorously, while Nurse Netta stared at us in consternation.

The Tower of London gave even greater opportunity for invention. I knew every inch of the ground and precincts before we were first taken there, walked without hesitation to stand by Traitors' Gate, and then pointed out, correctly, the name of every tower commanding the walls. Had I not beheaded Jeanne time and time again, with the crook of a walking stick, on Tower Green? I knew the identical spot where the block had stood. 'How nobly she walks to her death,' I heard one of the maids whisper as Jeanne strutted past, her curls pinned on the top of her head, while I, the axeman, dropped on one knee to ask her pardon before felling her with a single blow.

I was never myself in those days. I was whatever character (very often historical) that I was reading or interested in at the time. Later, when I started writing, the different characters became people on paper, that's all. Each book is a thing of the moment, a phase one is going through – just like our games were as children. When I am writing I have to become each person (though sometimes they surprise me). It's very like acting.

In 1916 we moved from 24 Cumberland Place (now Number 50) near Regents Park, where I was born, to Cannon Hall in Hampstead. I think Daddy must have been doing quite well at the time because he spent quite a bit on our new home. New furniture was bought and lots of pictures. 'George III's physician used to live here,' visitors would be told. Never mind George III's physician, it was the pictures that now decorated the wall up the big staircase that fascinated me – sad King Charles in profile came on the right-hand wall as one started to climb the stairs, and above him I remember, stretching the whole width of the wall, was a great battle scene, which could be enacted by us children again

Cannon Hall, circa 1921. It was the pictures Daddy bought to decorate the wall up the big staircase that fascinated me.

and again. At other times we would pretend to be characters from Shakespeare taken from the many prints scattered about the house, and then Daddy would join our games and encourage us, quoting long passages from the plays which he seemed to know by heart.

For our annual family holiday we'd take a house outside London – one year it was Denham, the next Croxley Green, then Slyfield near Stoke d'Abernon in Surrey. I remember Slyfield especially: Slyfield with the river Mole running through the garden, Slyfield with the big cedar tree on the lawn, Slyfield with the farm-buildings and the farm-animals alongside. Here at last was freedom. No longer the same London walks, day after day, routine that never varied; but instead space all around. We could run outside when we wanted and where we wanted, nurses did not scold so much in the country, maids were jollier, my mother did

Slyfield Manor, 1912. Great, old houses have always fascinated me. Someone once said that he couldn't think of a writer for whom houses have been so important an inspiration.

not wear a hat at lunch and say, 'Stop biting your nails' in that reproachful voice, Angela and I did not squabble.

The country . . . the country. 'She's a different child altogether out of London,' I heard someone say. Of course I was different. Here there were fields, trees, birds, animals. The farm men next door, Arthur and Tom, used to lift us on their great horses and take us round the yard. On our walks by the river we would come to a little gate. I must have been reading *Pilgrim's Progress* at the time, for this was the wicket gate through which Christian passed in the story. The muddied fields after rain could be the Slough of Despond, bushes and trees Vanity Fair, and the river itself the great divide at the end: 'And all the trumpets sounded for him on the other side.'

I loved the countryside but what really captured my imagination was the house. 'It's very old,' someone had said when we first went. 'They say the site is mentioned in Domesday. And in Tudor times Queen Elizabeth slept here.' Domesday had an ominous sound. And was Queen Elizabeth another Snow Queen waiting for us as I climbed the huge dark staircase to the murky landing above? Up, up, one step at a time, my heart thumping, while the staircase creaked. A picture of a man on the wall. I must not look at him or something terrible will happen. The landing at last, and pushing open a door I was through to a place of safety, I could hear voices, I was somehow in the bedroom that we used as a

night-nursery and Nurse was already tucking Jeanne up in her cot. Fear vanished. Domesday was no more. Queen Elizabeth had gone. Yet later, bath over, teeth brushed, rags in my hair and the light turned out, I was not so sure. The staircase would still be dark, the picture hanging on the wall, the shadows on the landing. Where had they all gone, the people who lived at Slyfield once? And where was I then? Who was I now?

It was about this time that Daddy became a fund of stories about his own past which sparked similar questions in my mind about our family and how I fitted in. He would take us up to New Grove House in Hampstead where he had lived as a boy. 'There's the studio,' he'd say. 'That's where Papa drew every day, he never minded us children playing around him. And there, behind the wall, is the small garden. You've seen the picture he drew of us, pretending to be trains, with Aunt Trixie leading, and myself the baby at the end.' Here was a new perspective, his past was my own past too. It all began to make sense. George du Maurier had come over to England from France as a young, virtually penniless artist, and become famous as an illustrator of the then influential *Punch* magazine. Later he had written three novels, of which the first, *Peter Ibbetson* – immensely popular in its day – was to exert a great influence on my life as a writer. We'd turn away from New Grove House and Daddy would point to Heath Mount, his first school, with schoolboys there still, wearing green caps. On to the White Stone pond, where he used to sail a boat, and into which Grandpapa had once jumped to save a drowning dog. 'That's the walk he took every morning, he had to walk to a certain spot and touch a tree there with his walking stick. If he forgot, it would be unlucky.' And one day, pointing to the fallen branch of what had once been a gnarled tree, Daddy said, 'Look, there's my armchair, I always called it my armchair and sat in it. It's still there.'

'I'm going to sit in it too,' I said and ran along to the branch and climbed into it, and yes, it was exactly like a chair. Daddy had sat there as a boy, about my age. And now he was a man. Where had the boy gone? It was haunting, queer. . . These places held a special meaning that I could feel, and when sometimes we'd continue our trek down to the parish churchyard where Grandpapa and Big Granny were buried, Aunt Sylvia in the grave alongside, Daddy would have tears in his eyes, so that one looked away. But he could never stay sad for long, soon he'd be laughing and joking again. But the dead relations in their graves, who had never meant very much to me, gradually became real and all of them young again, while the pictures that had made Grandpa famous – we had volumes of them, in a bookcase – became suddenly full of meaning. It awakened a family interest which was

George du Maurier. He started from nothing, came over from Paris with a few pounds in his pocket.

New Year's Day, 1920. *'I oversleep myself. We go for a long walk in the morning and stay indoors in the afternoon. It is my teddy-bear's birthday. I gave a party for her. Angela is very annoying. Jeanne and I box, and then I pretend I am a mid-shipman hunting slaves. Daddy says I have to stoop. I begin to read a book called* With Allenby in Palestine.*'*

Here was no budding woman ripe for sex instruction, but someone who had been left behind on the Never Never Island in Peter Pan!

more than family pride, a sense of continuity I suppose. Here were my roots, people whose experiences and ideas were a part of me.

I believe it was in the autumn of 1917, when air-raids had driven us to Cookham, that Mummy was invited by a friend of hers, Mrs Fitzwilliam, to bring us children for a visit to a house called Milton near Peterborough. We set off, one September day, by train. A car met us at Peterborough station, and after we had been driving for what seemed a long time the car passed through some lodge gates, and Mummy said, 'This is the park.' The park? This was nothing

Milton remains a childhood experience that was never surpassed. It became the inspiration, many years later, for Manderley, the house in Rebecca. The site was very much where Menabilly stands, but the interior, the rooms, the gallery, the 'feel' was all that I remembered of Milton.

like Regent's Park with flower beds and people strolling; these were fields or meadows, and nobody about.

'Do you mean it's private?' asked Angela.

'Of course,' my mother answered. 'The Fitzwilliam family have lived here for over four hundred years.'

This must mean 1500-and-something, I thought. Dates were still hazy. I couldn't remember who was King at that time, but for a family to go on in the same place year after year, being born, and getting married, and dying, was hard to believe. Suddenly the house was before us, long, grey-walled, stone, stretching endlessly, great windows set one upon the other with criss-cross window panes, then more stone, and columns, while to the left the building turned to form a sort of square, crowned by a clock-tower. Was this Milton?

Once inside, greetings were exchanged but what absorbed me was the magnificence of the great hall, the high ceiling, the panelled walls, and those portraits hanging upon them, men with lace collars, knee-breeches, coloured stockings, four centuries of Fitzwilliams. What memories were there here?

There was another visit to Milton the following spring, but both visits have merged to one memory. Unforgettable, unforgotten, Milton remains a childhood experience that was never surpassed. In later years, unconsciously and in dreams, Milton would fuse with Menabilly in far-off Cornwall. Milton, but in the setting of

Menabilly, became the inspiration of my most successful novel, *Rebecca*, but more about that later.

As child became adolescent I was more aware of the many visitors to our home in London. Sunday lunches with the dining room filled with guests from the world of theatre, were no longer the tiresome ordeal they had been once. Conversation with adults could be fun, and both my parents encouraged it. As little children we'd been very much a gang on our own, we'd think other children were rather silly. As we grew up I think we were always much more interested in older people if we were not just on our own, and we could be devils among them. Early on we'd been schooled in the du Maurier skill of satire, and frequently towards the end of Sunday lunch, we'd come into our own. Mother would say, 'Coffee? Black or white?'. We had this thing you see, that if any man had milk in his coffee we'd think it was a sign that he was effeminate, and we'd sit, waiting, eyeing each other across the table, and when some poor inoffensive man said, 'White,' we'd nudge each other and convulse with laughter.

The adored Gladys Cooper – a frequent visitor – and her young son John became my favourite people outside the family. Indeed, with shared holidays, I looked upon both as family and loved them equally. The actor Basil Rathbone was another popular visitor – he had performed as the hero in the stage adaptation of Grandpapa's novel, *Peter Ibbetson*. There is a page in my diaries, which I began keeping from the age of thirteen, on which I had drawn a heart, pierced by an arrow, and the words, 'I love Basil' scribbled upon it. I wonder what I should have said if I had known that over twenty years later he would act the part of wicked Lord Rockingham in the film adaptation of *Frenchman's Creek*!

I remember too my friend and exact contemporary Frances Lonsdale, daughter of Daddy's great friend the dramatist Freddie Lonsdale (and later to become the author Frances Donaldson), and how we shared a childhood confidence that one day we would both become writers. We were quite serious, for one Christmas, when we were both about thirteen, we collaborated on a play we called *The Sacrifice* and performed it in front of those veterans of the real theatre Sir Squire and Lady Bancroft.

Meanwhile my reading continued apace, and in 1923 when I was sixteen I noted in my diary that books read 'averaged nine a month'. Dickens, Browning, George Eliot, Scott, Thackeray, Galsworthy, Samuel Johnson, Sheridan's plays, Wilde, the Brontës. These and others crowd the pages of my diaries. Wilde filled many reading hours that year, winning the highest marks. *Beyond* by Galsworthy was pronounced 'wonderful', while Ethel M

Dell's *Charles Rex* was 'soppy tosh'. Strangely my first encounter with the Brontë sisters produced no more than 'charming' for *Jane Eyre* and 'very good' for *Wuthering Heights*. Readers of this present book may find many ways in which my early life affected my later work, but looking back now I can see clearly how my reading influenced me in more than a general way. For example, *Jane Eyre* must have influenced me directly with *Rebecca* and R L Stevenson with *Jamaica Inn*, even though I read *Treasure Island* when I was eight. So many things sink into the unconscious as a child and well up later.

As a teenager, the most indelible impression was made by the beautifully crafted stories of Katherine Mansfield who, had I but known it, lived with husband John Middleton Murray not five minutes away from Cannon Hall. I felt instinctively that if I could only one day write some sketch that might compare, however humbly, to Katherine Mansfield's, then I need not despair.

Poems and stories began to flow from my pen, but they were rarely finished. It was a time of great enthusiasm but somehow something was missing. I was in a thoroughly privileged position – there was an endless stream of writers and actors flowing through our lives at the time – and my imagination was teeming with ideas, but still I found it so much easier to think out stories vaguely in my mind than to set them down in words. How on earth did Daddy's friend Edgar Wallace manage to turn out a book a week? 'If only I can stick at it,' says my diary, 'and eventually make some money.'

An incident – strangely relevant – comes to mind. When Miss Torrance, our first governess, came to teach us – I must have been all of four years old – she asked me if I could write. I turned to her and said, 'Yes, I have written a book.'

'What is it called?'

'It's called *John, in the Wood of the World*.'

It was not true of course. I could barely turn pot-hooks into capitals let alone form sentences to write a book. So why say it? Showing off, no doubt. But what on earth made me choose such a title? Freud has a good deal to say about dreaming of finding yourself in a forest, and in the literary tradition the wood or forest symbolises mental or spiritual confusion. Many writers have used the symbol and it goes back at least as far as Dante's 14th-century *Divine Comedy* in which, at the very beginning he comes out of the forest and sees the mountain; coming out of the forest is his first awakening, if you like. The hero of my non-existent story was evidently similarly lost, surrounded by trees. Whether he found his way to the light or remained in darkness I shall never discover, but in some curious way I had chosen as the title of my first imaginative 'work' a metaphor that was peculiarly appropriate to

1926. *'I would like to go out and live my life in some new colony, where things are just starting, new. Somewhere away from decadence, and modern materialism.'*

the struggles of this writer through her teens.

I was, however, prevented from being too self-obsessed by an intellectually exhilarating spell at finishing school outside Paris, at Camposena, near Meudon, after which I decided I had somehow to change my life. I was nineteen years of age and had developed this strong desire to be independent, to break free. Angela seemed perfectly happy living at home, with masses of friends, in and out of the theatre world, never at a loss for something to do. And

Jeanne was equally happy at her Hampstead day-school, developing a new prowess in hockey and also making a circle of friends. But my diary reads: 'I would like to go out and live my life in some new colony, where things are just starting, new. Somewhere away from decadence, and modern materialism. Away from Europe. Perhaps South Africa, a farm, where there would be no town life, and plenty of riding. I can see myself in my mind's eye, free. . .'

You may wonder at the implacability of this child who had so much, but my unsettledness was not born of perversity or any antagonism to family. The child destined to be a writer is vulnerable to every wind that blows. Now warm, now chill, next joyous, then despairing, the essence of his nature is to escape the atmosphere about him, no matter how stable, even loving. No ties, no binding chains, save those he forges for himself. I did not know then that escape can be delusion, and what the writer is running from is not the enclosing world and its inhabitants, but his own inadequate self that fears to meet the demands which life makes upon it. Therefore create. Act God. Fashion men and women as Prometheus fashioned them from clay, and by doing this work out the unconscious strife within and be reconciled. While in others, imbued with a desire to mould, to instruct, to spread a message that will inspire the reader and so change his world, the motive may be humane and even noble (many great works have done this), the source is the same, *dissatisfaction* – a yearning to escape.

I must have told Jeanne about my dreams of rounding up sheep and cattle on a farm, because one day she announced that a friend

Looking towards Derwent Fells at the southern point of Lake Derwentwater. The farm where we stayed was set high in the hills across the bridge, beyond the settlement.

of hers knew of a farm in Cumberland, near Lake Derwentwater, where they took lodgers, and what fun it would be if we could go for a few weeks in the Easter holidays. Greatly to our delight, my mother approved of the idea, and on April 7th, 1926, she, Jeanne, Jock (my dog) and I caught the 10.35 from Euston to Keswick, arriving at our destination some time after 7 o'clock in the evening. A kindly Mrs Clarke welcomed us at the farm, set high in the hills the other side of Derwentwater, my mother approved of the rooms, and we sat down to a hot supper in the sitting room, in front of a blazing fire.

Mountains, woods, valleys, farms – earlier holidays in the South of France, in Algiers, in Dieppe, could not compare with this, my first experience of rugged scenery, of running water coursing through the hills down to the lake, and the names of those hills – Cat Bells, Causey Pike. No skipping up them, as I had seen myself, but a steady jog, pausing for breath, and Jock – perhaps owing to his West Highland blood – truly in his element.

Walks and excursions filled our time, one of the excursions being

Earlier holidays could not compare with this my first experience of rugged scenery, of running water coursing through the hills down to the lake.

The lakes themselves, mysterious, often shrouded in mist.

to Dove Cottage, Grasmere, where Wordsworth had lived. Seeing his personal things, his desk, just as they had been when he was alive and writing there, impressed me deeply. And the lakes themselves – 'mysterious, often shrouded in mist, and with little islands upon them like the island in Mary Rose', I noted in my diary – and the people, our farming family the Clarkes, so honest, so true. 'How different from everyone in London,' I wrote. 'There is nothing artifical here, no insincerity, no falseness. If their only interest is in farming, then this is real. I love them. I love them all.' This was all so different from the world that I knew – a real awakening – a feeling for the countryside as opposed to the city, primitive, elemental, a desire for roots in the soil. . .

My return to London did not, however, see a change for the better in my efforts to write. On the contrary, 'I wrote better at fifteen than I do now,' I grumbled in my diary after glancing through some scraps. 'Perhaps if I changed from fiction to sociology I should do better. A treatise on civilisation? It might be good practice for style if nothing else.'

The truth was that any excuse served to lay down my pen or much-bitten pencil. Edgar Wallace, his wife Jim and daughter Pat, were ever forward with invitations, Ascot amongst them. There was Wimbledon with my mother, and after the first night of a Noel Coward play we picked up Gerald from the theatre and went on to a 'small, smart party at the Victor Pagets, with a good band, and Jack Smith sang, and I danced with the Prince of Wales! Nice, but rather a pathetic figure. Didn't get home till half-past four.'

Then in mid-July (the same year, 1926) I set forth to Trébeurden in Brittany with Fernande, whose finishing school I had attended in France and who was now simply my friend. There I would swim every day, climb rocks and go for long walks. Excursions along the coast by char-a-banc were exciting, stimulating, and farms in South Africa were quite forgotten. I must live by the sea, somewhere on the coast of Brittany, where there would be rocks to climb and pools to comb, and I could bathe naked, with nobody by. Perhaps an island would be the thing? There was an island off Trébeurden, the Isle of Molène. I used to stare at it with longing, for it was uninhabited. . . Yes, an island. But perhaps not Brittany, maybe Greece. I didn't know. . . But the sea must be close, there had to be the sea.

When I arrived home at the end of August everyone told me how well I looked, and that it was evident that living by the sea suited me. 'We have been thinking,' my mother said, 'that it would be a good idea if we could find somewhere, a home of our own, perhaps in Cornwall, where we could all go for holidays, instead of abroad. Edgar [Wallace] has been so generous over *The Ringer* that we could afford it. You'd like that, wouldn't you? Lots of swimming and walking.' *The Ringer* had met with great success at Wyndham's and as my father had not only produced it but contributed much of the dialogue, Edgar had generously shared his royalties with him.

So it was that on September 13th, 1926, my mother and the three of us – Angela, Jeanne and myself – set off for Cornwall in search of a holiday home.

CHAPTER TWO

A NEW AWAKENING

~

The hired car swept round the curve of the hill, and suddenly the full expanse of Fowey harbour was spread beneath us. The contrast between this sheet of wide water, the nearby jetties, the moored ships, the grey roofs of Fowey across the way, the clustering cottages of Polruan on the opposite hill by the harbour mouth, and narrow, claustrophobic Looe where we had spent the

Suddenly the full expanse of Fowey harbour was spread beneath us.

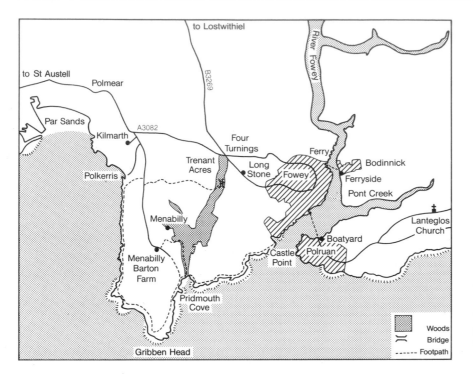

Bodinnick, as I saw her for the first time. Ferryside (at the time called Swiss Cottage) is on the right of the picture. The sign of the Ferry Inn is almost visible on the wall across the road, a little further up the hill.

night on our way down from London was astonishing, like the gateway to another world.

My spirits soared.

The car deposited my mother, Angela, me and Jeanne at the foot of the hill by the ferry. We could either cross the ferry to Fowey or lunch first at the Ferry Inn here in Bodinnick. It was nearly one o'clock, and we chose the latter course. Before climbing the hill to lunch our eyes were caught by a board saying 'For Sale' on a gate just above the ferry. Behind the gate was a rough piece of ground and a house by the water's edge, a strange looking house, built like a Swiss chalet. 'Yes,' said the ferryman standing near by, 'they call it Swiss Cottage. They used to build boats there, down under, and have the second floor for lofts. The top floor was for living. It's for sale right enough.'

We went to the inn for lunch and afterwards during coffee, our mother talked with the proprietor, enquiring first about lodgings on the opposite side in Fowey (pronounced Foy). We were touring Cornwall, she explained, with the idea of looking for a house for the holidays; we came from Hampstead, London . . .

I was too impatient to wait for the conversation to drag on. I jerked my head to the others to follow me, leaving my mother

I would wake in the morning and go to the window, and stare out across the harbour. Another ship had come to anchor during the night – what was her name? Where was she from?

talking. We went down the hill. My sisters tried the gate by the ferry and went into the yard. I found another gate, and a pathway leading to the other side of the house. Here there was a garden, or what went for a garden, terraced uphill, tier upon tier, and the chalet part of the house thrust itself forward, built, so it seemed, against the rock, with the windows facing straight out across the harbour. I went and stood beneath the chalet, the water immediately beneath me, and looked towards the harbour mouth. There were small boats everywhere, and yachts at anchor, but more stirring still a big ship was drawing near, with two attendant tugs, to moor a few cables' length from the house itself. There was a smell in the air of tar and rope and rusted chain, a smell of tidal water. Down harbour, around the point, was the open sea.

Fowey harbour today, from Pont Creek above Polruan.

Ferryside as it may be seen today at Bodinnick. There, sitting in my bedroom above the figurehead of the schooner Jane Slade, I began to write my first novel.

Here was the freedom I desired, long sought-for, not yet known. Freedom to write, to walk, to wander, freedom to climb hills, to pull a boat, to be alone. One feature of my excitement was the feeling that it could not be mere chance that brought us to the ferry. It seemed so right.

Swiss Cottage was bought and re-named Ferryside (to us the name had horrid associations with an underground railway station in the Finchley Road at home, in London). Throughout winter and spring it was put in the hands of decorators and builders, and on May 14th, 1927, the day after my twentieth birthday, my mother and Angela, who had come with me to see the transformation, returned to London, leaving me on my own for the first time in my life.

Why was it, I used to wonder, that being on my own in Hampstead plunged me, too often, into a fit of depression? Work in the garage-room – where I tried to write – a toil. Walks on the heath so tame. A general dissatisfaction of mind and body. Yet here in Fowey it was like being someone else. I was never for one moment bored, never depressed.

Oh, the happiness of those first weeks! The thrill of crossing

Oh, the happiness of those weeks! The thrill of crossing backwards and forwards on the ferry never palled.

backwards and forwards on the ferry never palled. To stand on the Fowey side, at Passage slip, and shout 'Over!', and after a moment or two to see the cheery wave from the ferry man at Bodinnick, or better still, if a cart had to be transported, to cry, 'Horse-boat!' – none of your car ferries more than half-a-century ago.

Everyone in the village was so friendly. I soon got to know their names. The Swigges, the Couches, the Bunneys, the Hunkins up the road, little Miss Roberts waving from her cottage, her Macaw Robert calling 'Rob, Rob!' from the sea wall, old Captain Bate from across the harbour, who lent me a book called Gypsy of the Horn in which he had figured as the skipper.

I would awake of a morning and go to the window, and stare out across the harbour. Another ship had come to anchor during the night – what was her name? Where was she from? Fowey has always been a terrific port for the china clay trade – ships come from all over the world to load up at the jetties, and I became friendly with many of the seamen, drinking tea with them, listening to their stories. I remember one ship in particular, the Wearbridge. I would call out and wave to the skipper, Captain Richie Bird (Dickie Bird!), when the Wearbridge passed my window at Ferryside, and he would give a terrific hoot in return.

Then of course there was Adams, a veteran of Jutland, who taught me how to steer a boat in a rough sea and not go on the rocks, how to take a hook out of a fish's mouth without squirming. We would fish for conger-eel up by the jetties after dark, and go

When the men came back from their fishing, they would lean over the wall by the slip and gossip over their pipes, the nets spread out to dry on the cobbled stones. However far away a Cornishman sails from Fowey, he remains rooted to his homeland as surely as the trees in the shelter of Lerryn woods.

Adams and I would fish for conger-eel up the jetties. I think I must have been born into the wrong atmosphere – 'The real me is at Fowey,' I wrote in my diary, 'not London where everyone fusses. All I want is Fowey.'

rabbiting together when winter came.

One day, on one of my walks up Pont Creek, an estuary of the Fowey that separates the two villages of Bodinnick and Polruan, I came upon a derelict schooner, called *Jane Slade*. She lay there on the mud flats, abandoned to die, her hulk rotting but her colourful figurehead proudly challenging the passage of time. I used to visit her often, climbing aboard and imagining what seas she had once travelled, what her history had been, who the men were that had

One day on one of my walks up Pont Creek, I came upon a derelict schooner. She lay there on the mud-flats, abandoned to die. I used to visit her often, climbing aboard and imagining what seas she had once travelled, what her history had been, who the men were that had manned her now all dead and gone . . . I discovered that the schooner's name was Jane Slade. *She became the inspiration of my first novel,* The Loving Spirit.

manned her, now all dead and gone, and I wrote a poem about her called *The Old Ship*.

> *No battered hulk am I!*
> *No coward timorous of wind or gale,*
> *Have I not ridden seas and carried sail*
> *Beyond the dreams of man, away, away*
> *Down in the haunted latitudes where lay*
> *Cold lands unvisited? O! tell me why*
> *They leave me here so desolate and sore.*
> *Far from the sea – far from the wind-swept shore,*
> *To die – To die!*

The first line owes a debt to Emily Brontë's poem *Last Lines*, which begins, 'No coward soul is mine', but the rest is D du M and nobody else! The voice of Jane calls out 'Why do they leave the water in my hold? Why is the wound not tended in my side?' and the poem bemoans the fate of this once proud vessel now left in limbo, denied the dignity of a final resting place at sea.

> *Loose my bonds – set me free –*
> *Let me rise from my bed –*
> *Let me go to the sea!*
> *O! the sound of the sea.*

I can hear the scattering of the sand
Upon the beach.
I can see the shattering of the waves
And the screech
Of the wild wet wind upon the land.

One day I asked Adams about the schooner and discovered that the figurehead was a carving of a real woman. Jane Slade had been the mother of the men who built the vessel at the boatyard at Polruan. What's more, Adams told me that his wife had been a Slade, a grand-daughter of the original Jane. 'There are stacks of old letters in a box,' he went on, 'all about the family, and when the schooner was built. We'll look at them one day.' Some time later he took me to meet the man who then owned the Polruan boatyard, one Ernie Slade. Not only had Jane been his gran, but his uncle Tom was the old schooner's skipper and the hulk itself was at last to be broken up. 'Would you like to have the figurehead?'

And so the colourful carving came to rest on the beam outside my bedroom window at Ferryside. My interest in the family took me up to Lanteglos churchyard, high above the creek, to find where Jane had been buried, and sure enough there was the family tombstone – Christopher Slade and his wife Jane Symons, died

Below: *My interest in the Slade family took me up to Lanteglos churchyard to find where Jane had been buried, and sure enough there was the family tombstone.*

Left: *The Slade boatyard. Jane was mother of the men who built the derelict schooner. She became Janet Coombe in* The Loving Spirit: *'Often Janet would wander down to the shipbuilding yard . . . she loved the great trunks of trees, old and well seasoned, that lay waiting to be cut for planks.'*

1885, aged seventy-two. Then Adams came along with his big box of letters and papers about the family, and I went through them that very same evening, faded handwriting, going back to the early part of the nineteenth century. They had about them a personal touch; it was almost as though I had opened up a coffin and looked upon the dead.

The following day I couldn't get them out of my head. I realised that there was enough material here for a book. Ernie Slade supplied more information, and soon I was busy drawing out a genealogical table of the whole family down to the present day. Was it my fancy, or was it true that Jane dominated them all, even after death – and she would be getting on when the schooner was built. . . Poems and short stories were pushed aside, I could think of nothing but Jane Slade.

I began the novel, my first, on a terrible wild day in October with a howling sou'westerly wind and slashing rain, a rug wrapped around my knees, sitting at the desk in my bedroom at Ferryside. Its title, *The Loving Spirit*, like the first line of *The Old Ship*, came from a poem by Emily Brontë. The Slades became the Coombe family – Jane Slade became Janet Coombe – and Polruan became Plyn.

'Janet leant against the castle ruins with the sea at her feet . . . Then she closed her eyes, and the jumbled thoughts fled from her mind . . . she was possessed with the strange power and clarity of the moon itself.'

The discovery of the schooner and research into the family that built her gave me the story, but my interest in the Slade family was really only the vehicle for what had at last made me sit down and write a full-length work. I have often taken letters, family papers, archive material, and on one occasion someone else's unfinished novel, and breathed new life into them. But this process – though literally a process of inspiration – is quite different to what inspires the creative process. The inspiration to write a novel comes from within, and more than any of my others *The Loving Spirit* was inspired by the sense of freedom that my new existence at Ferryside brought.

A short story may arise from a single incident, in my case very often an incident I have witnessed while travelling. There will be a brewing process in the mind, as with a novel, but a full-length novel cuts deeper into one's emotional life. Something begins to well up inside you; it's irrepressible. Some dim sort of facet of the novel begins to well up in your own life. It's a bit like having a baby, it grows inside you, it is an aspect of you, a second self. Then the time comes to sit down in front of the typewriter. When it's over you're purged and you feel a terrific sensation of relief, and then empty until the nagging feeling begins again. The metaphor is especially apt in the case of *The Loving Spirit*, which is the story of how Janet Coombe realises her dream of true freedom through the birth of her third son, Joseph.

One night when *The Loving Spirit* was still in embryo, scarcely born in thought, I walked up to Castle Point. The moon was high in the sky, and there was no sound but the moan of the still water lapping the rocks beyond the harbour. It seemed to me that I was standing on the cliffs years hence with a grown-up son. I was a ghost, long dead, existing only in his thoughts. And from that I passed on to thinking about my unborn book. My thoughts were of a past and future no longer separated in time, and I knew it must be the story of four generations.

Down harbour, round the point, was the open sea. Here was the freedom I desired, long sought-for, not yet known. Freedom to write, to walk, to wander, freedom to climb hills, to pull a boat, to be alone.

Janet leant against the Castle ruins with the sea at her feet, and the light of the moon on her face. Then she closed her eyes, and the jumbled thoughts fled from her mind, her tired body seemed to slip away from her, and she was possessed with the strange power and clarity of the moon itself. When she opened her eyes for a moment there was a mist about her, and when it dissolved she saw kneeling beside the cliff with his head bowed in his hands, the figure of a man. She knew that he was filled with wild despair and bitterness, and that his poor lost soul was calling to her for comfort.

She went and knelt beside him, and held his head to her breast, while she stroked his grey hair with her hand.

Then he looked up at her, his wild brown eyes crazy with fear at himself.

And she knew him to belong to the future, when she was dead and in her grave, but she recognised him as her own.

'Hush, my sweet love, hush, and cast away your fear. I'm beside you always, always, an' there's none who'll harm you.'

'Why didn't you come before?' he whispered, holding her close. 'They've been trying to take me away from you, and the whole world is black and filled with devils. There's no truth, dearest, no path for me to take. You'll help me, won't you?'

'We'll suffer and love together,' she told him. 'Every joy, and sorrow in your mind an' body is mine too. A path will show itself soon, then the shadows clear away from your spirit.'

'I've heard your whispers often, and hearkened to your blessed words of comfort. We've talked with one another too, alone in the silence of the sea, on the decks of the ship that is part of you. Why have you never come before, to hold me like this, and to feel my head beside your heart?'

'I don't understand,' she said. 'I don't know where we come from, nor how the mist was broken for me to get to you; I heard you callin', and there's nothing kept me back.'

'They've been long weary days since you went from me, an' I've not heeded your counsel, nor deserved your trust in me,' he told her. 'See how I'm old now, with the grey hairs in my head and beard, and you younger than I ever knew you, with your pale girl's face and your tender unworn hands.'

'I have no reckoning in my mind of what is past, nor that which is to be,' said she, 'but all I know is there's no space of time here, nor in our world, nor any world hereafter. There be no separation for us, no beginnin' and no end – we'm cleft together you an' I, like the stars to the sky.' Then he said: 'They whisper amongst themselves I'm mad, my love, my reason's gone and there's danger in my eyes. I can feel the blackness creepin' on me, and when it comes for good, I'll neither see you nor feel you – and there'll be nothin' left here but desolation and despair.'

He shuddered and trembled as a cloud passed over the face of the moon, and it seemed to her he was a child in her arms crying for comfort.

'Never fear, when the black fit seizes you, I'll hold you as I hold you now,' she soothed him. 'When you can neither see nor hear, and you're fightin' with yourself, I'll be at your side and strivin' for you.'

He threw back his head and watched her as she stood, white against the sky with a smile on her lips.

'You're an angel tonight,' he said, 'standing at the gates of Heaven before the birth of Christ. It's Christmas, and they're singing the hymn in Lanoc Church.'

'Fifty years or a thousand years, it's all the same,' said Janet. 'Our comin' here together is the proof of it.'

'You'll never leave me again, then?' he asked.

'Never no more.'

He knelt and kissed her foot-prints in the snow.

'Tell me, is there a God?'

He looked into her eyes and read the truth.

They stood for a minute and gazed at each other, seeing themselves as they never would on earth. She saw a man, bent and worn, with wild unkempt hair and weary eyes; he saw a girl, young and fearless, with the moonlight on her face.

'Good night, my mother, my beauty, my sweet.'

'Good night, my love, my baby, my son.'

Then the mist came between them, and hid them from one another.

Time and again in the novel Janet climbs to Castle Point to be 'nearer to something for which there was no name.' Here, 'where things have no reckoning of time', Janet perceives the fate – long distant – of her unborn son. It seemed that this hillside was our own world, hers and mine, a small planet of strange clarity and understanding. There was a freedom here, a freedom that was part of the air and the sea; like the glad tossing of the leaves in autumn, and the shy fluttering wings of a bird.

Janet longs for freedom as I had longed for it; a throb of intense

A throb of intense pain shook her being when she saw a ship leave the harbour at Plyn, her sails spread to the wind, and move away like a silent phantom across the face of the sea.

pain would shake her being when she saw a ship leave the harbour of Plyn, her sails spread to the wind, moving away like a silent phantom across the face of the sea. Something would tear at her heart to be gone too, to be part of the ship, part of the seas and the sky above, with the glad free ways of a gull. She loved her husband Thomas dearly, but she knew in her soul there was something waiting for her greater than this.

The damp still weather changed of a sudden one afternoon, great purple clouds gathered from the south-west, and a low ugly line ran along the sea's horizon. With the turn of the tide the strong wind changed to a gale, and descended with all its force upon Plyn.

High mountainous seas broke against the rocks at the harbour mouth, and swept their way inside the entrance. The spray came up over the Castle ruins, and the water rose above the level of the town quay, flooding the ground floor of the cottages grouped there on the cobbled square.

The men shut their women folk inside their houses, and made their way to the harbour slip, to see to the safety of their boats. It was the last day of October, 'All Hallowe'en', and usually a beacon was lit on this night, and the custom followed of feeding it at midnight with driftwood, and then proceeding through the town, but tonight this was abandoned – for no one would venture forth into such a gale unless on duty bound.

Thomas Coombe was down at the yard, watching the rising tide with apprehension and longing for the turn, when no more damage could be done. At Ivy House the children were put to bed and already asleep in spite of the howling wind. Janet had laid the supper and was awaiting Thomas's return.

The rain had now ceased, only the wind and the sea shouted in unison. Every leaf was scattered, and the broken branches swung in the trees, creaking and shaking like the rattle of a ship's shroud. Something was dashed against the window and fell, sending Janet's hand to her side with the shock of the sound. She opened the window to see, and saw the dead body of a gull with its two wings broken.

The wild air tore at her curtains and blew to darkness the flickering candles. The fire hissed and shrank in the grate. Then Janet felt the movement of the live thing stir within her, she felt the striving of one who would break his bonds and be free.

And to her, too, came the call for liberty, the last desperate longing of a soul to seek its freedom, and the anguish of a body cast from its restraint.

She threw up her hands and cried aloud, and the wild mocking wind echoed her cry – 'Come with me,' called the voice out of the darkness, 'come and seek your destiny on the everlasting hills.'

So Janet wrapped her shawl about her head, and conscious only of the pain that gripped her and the struggle of spirit and body, she stumbled away into the wild wet wind, with the call of the thundering sea in her ears.

Down in the yard Thomas and his men watched the slackening of the tide, and when they saw it retreat slowly inch by inch, angry at the forces which compelled it, they knew that the premises were safe for the night until the following morning.

'Well, lads, it's been a hard forbiddin' watch for us. What do ye say to a cup o' somethin' hot up to the house? The wife will have it ready and waitin'.'

The men thanked him gratefully, and marched by his side up the hill to Ivy House, half bent with the weight of the wind at their backs.

'Hullo, no lights,' said Thomas. 'She's surely never gone to bed.'

He made his way into the house, the men at his heels.

The room was just as Janet had left it, with supper on the table, but the fire was low in the grate, and the candles blown out.

'That's queer,' muttered Thomas, ''tesn't like Janie to leave a room in such a state.'

One of the men looked over his shoulders.

'Seems as if Mrs Coombe left everythin' hasty-like,' he said. 'Suppose she's been took bad, she's very near her time, isn't she, Mr Thomas, beggin' your pardon?'

Fear clutched at the heart of Thomas.

'Wait,' he said, 'I'll see what she's about.'

He went to the bedroom over the porch and opened the door.

'Janie,' he called, 'Janie, where are you to?'

Samuel and his sister were sleeping sound, there was no movement in the

'There'd be a moon over the water, like a path of silver, leading away from the black sea to the sky.'

house. Thomas ran downstairs, breathing hard.

'She's not there,' he stammered, 'she's not anywhere; she's not in the house.'

The men looked grave, they read the fear in his eyes. Suddenly he clutched at the table for support, his legs weakening. 'She's gone to the cliffs,' he cried, 'she's gone out into the gale, crazy with the pain.'

He seized the lantern in his hands and ran from the house, shouting and calling to the men to follow him.

Folk came to their doors. 'What's all the pother an' noise?'

'Janet Coombe's trouble is upon her, an' she's gone to the cliffs to lose herself,' came the cry.

Men donned their coats and found lanterns to join in the search, and one or two women besides, sorrowful and anxious at the thought that one of their kind should suffer. The group staggered up the hill after Thomas, already a long way ahead.

Borne through the air came the chime of midnight from Lanoc Church, the final notes loud and triumphant with a gust of wind.

'All Hallowe'en,' whispered the folk amongst themselves, 'and the dead risin' from their graves to walk the earth, an' the evil spirits of all time fillin' the air.'

And they huddled close together and called for God's mercy and protection, with horror in their hearts for the plight of Janet.

They gathered beside Thomas at the summit of the cliff, where the gale nigh shook them from their feet, and the black sea crashed against the rocks.

Hither and thither tossed the pale lanterns, searching the ground. 'Janie,' cried Thomas, 'Janie – Janie, answer me.'

No sign of her on the bare grass, no sign of her in the tangled ferns.

Now the rain came once again, blinding the eyes of the searchers, the boiling waves dashed themselves to pieces, sending cloud after cloud of stinging spray on to the cliffs above.

The wind tore at the ground and the trees, wailing and sobbing, and cried like a thousand wild devils let loose in the air.

Then a faint shout came from Thomas, who held his lantern high above his head, and the light fell slantways upon the figure of Janet beside the Castle ruin.

She was crouched half kneeling in the grass, her hands flung out and clenched, her head thrown back. Her clothes were drenched with the spray and the rain, and her long dark hair fell wild about her face.

On her cheeks were the marks of her own tears, and those of the rain from Heaven.

Her teeth were biting into her torn lips, and blood ran at the corner of her mouth. The light in her eyes was savage, primitive, the light of the first animal who walked the earth, and the first woman who knew pain.

Thomas knelt by the side of Janet, and took her in his arms, and carried her away down the bleak hillside into the town of Plyn, and so to her home and laid her on the bed.

All the night the storm raged, but when at length the wind ceased, and the sea quietened its mournful clamour, peace came to her.

And when Janet held her wailing baby to her breast, with his wild dark

Marie-Louise, *my first sailing boat, a fishing lugger – 32 feet overall, a 12-foot beam, 5 foot 6 inches deep, rigged as a yawl. She was built at Slade's yard just as the* Janet Coombe *would be.*

eyes and his black hair, she knew that nothing in the whole world mattered but this, that he for whom she had been waiting had come at last.

For mother and son, it was like a union of spirit defying time and eternity – something that had existed between them before birth. Joseph was Janet's second self. He loved the sea and the ships with the same passion that she did. In imagination she would do, through Joseph, all the things which had been denied her because she had been born a woman.

Although he was only seven, Joe was tall and big for his age, nearly as tall as Samuel who was eleven. As he stood there, with his dark eyes fixed on his father's, his head thrown back and his chin in the air, he looked so much like his mother that Thomas turned away for a moment . . . he hardened himself.

'Do you know you're a bad evil boy?'

The child made no answer.

'Baint you goin' to reply to your father when he asks you a question? Say you'm sorry at once, will ye?'

'I'll says I'm sorry when you gives me my boat, an' not afore,' said the boy coolly, and he stuck his small hands in his breeches and tried to whistle.

His defiance staggered Thomas. Never had Samuel behaved like this, or either little Herbert or Philip, the two youngest boys. Only Joseph persisted in getting his own way above them all, as if there was something in him that made him different to the others. He looked different too, with his dark wild appearance; his clothes were always in holes and his boots through at the toe.

Two or three times a week he played truant from school, or was complained of in some way or other, generally for fighting. It seemed as if Thomas had no authority over him at all. Only Janet knew how to handle him. Since his birth seven years ago on that dark October night, this small bit of a lad had dominated the household. He had needed more careful rearing than either Samuel or Mary, and during the first few months of his existence the house had rung with his screams and his yells. There had never been such a baby for making a noise. Only when his mother held him close to her and whispered to him, was he quietened. Once he grew out of his babyhood he threw off his first temporary frailty, and developed into a strong sturdy boy. Ivy House was seldom still or peaceful now, it resounded with either his laughter or his rages. He was not spoilt, there was no attempt made to pamper or give in to him in any way, it was just the boy's personality that threw a sort of glamour about him, and there was no gainsaying him . . .

'I'm not goin' to stay i' the yard 'longside o' father, with Sammie an' Herbie,' he said. 'I'm goin' to be a sailor like I've told you many a time. And when I'm Master o' my ship – *Janet Coombe*'s her name – you'll be with me – at my side facin' the danger an' the wonder of it. Promise you'll come – promise?'

He took her chin in his hands.

She closed her eyes.

'I promise.'

'Do you know my ship will be the fleetest ship in Plyn – an' in the bows of her, flauntin' the world with her eyes an' her mouth, there'll be your figurehead.'

Janet knelt with him pressed close against her.

Into both their minds came the vision of a ship with her white sails spread. Joseph laughing with the wind in his face, and in the bows of the vessel, her hands clasped to her breast and her head thrown back – the figurehead of Janet.

'Will you be proud?' whispered the boy.

Lanteglos Church, above Pont Creek, where I made thanks when the final word of The Loving Spirit *was written. 'If it was Sunday the bells from Lanoc Church called the folk of Plyn to evensong, and the people would walk along the footpath that led over the fields to the Church above Polmear.'*

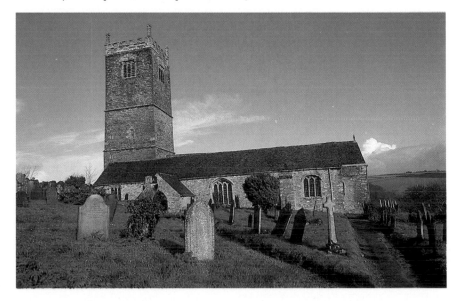

She raised her head and looked into his eyes.

With the development of his character he seemed to open also that of his mother's. From the moment of his birth Janet had altered. The soft pliability of temperament that had obeyed Thomas's wishes during the first years of marriage had flown to the winds, and with it the solitary melancholy part of her that had seized her later. She had emerged stronger, braver, utterly fearless in mind, soul, and body, with no humble wishes to please her husband only and to care for his home, and no half-conscious longing and vague desires in her mind.

Thursday, March 30th, 1930. 'At last! The final stroke has been drawn, the final word written, and *The Loving Spirit* is finished. The relief to have done it is enormous. I was so excited I could hardly eat my lunch. In the afternoon I went over to Lanteglos church to make some sort of thanksgiving, and to visit the tombstone of Jane Slade. If Michael Joseph of Curtis Brown [my agent] tells me he doesn't like it, or I must rewrite, he can go to hell. I can't go back to it any more.

'The future faces me with doubt and perplexity. "No coward soul is mine"?'

I can't remember exactly how well *The Loving Spirit* sold, but after its publication I had my independence; like Janet I was in control. I could come down to Fowey when I liked, do what I liked and pay for myself. My independence, and all that it implied, had been my main object always. The driving force was that I must write, get this story out of my system, but following closely upon that, I must be free. The one led to the other. And in the end, Joseph would give Janet her freedom too:

She was to be carvel-built with a square stern, and the length of her was ninety-seven feet. Her main breadth was twenty-two feet, and her depth, a little over twelve feet. Thomas and his sons reckoned that when she was finished she would be about a hundred and sixty tons gross. She was to be rigged as a two-masted top-sail schooner. A great moment it was when the framework of her was finished, and she stood with her mighty ribs waiting to be planked. Then every man in the yard was summoned to the work, and Plyn resounded with the ceaseless hammer and crash as the nails were driven into the sturdy planks.

Janet stood over them, a smile on her lips, a hand on her hips, a tall, lithe figure for all her fifty years. Should any man down his tools, it was: 'Were ye weak when your mother cradled ye, my lad, to give way so soon?' and the fellow would glance up ashamed and meet her keen unwavering eye. There was no standing against her, and no one cared to, for that matter, for she had a way with her that it was impossible to resist.

Unknown to Plyn and herself, however, the strength of her heart declined day by day. As the ship, her namesake, took shape and became a thing of strength, so did Janet's body weaken and her pulse slacken.

She could scarce drag herself to the top of the hill now without a faintness

Left: *The men of Slade's Boatyard, a photograph two years after Jane Slade died in 1885. A young Ernie Slade is first from left on the bottom row, but incredibly – seated furthest right on that row – is the hero of the novel himself, Joseph Slade (Joseph Coombe).*

Below: *Slade's Boatyard at Polruan. After the war we bought the yard and Tommy, my husband, had his own boat built there. It is now the property of C Toms & Son (Boatbuilders and Engineers).*

Left: *'A great moment it was when the framework of her was finished and she stood with her mighty ribs waiting to be planked.'*

coming upon her, without strange black shadows dancing before her eyes. She took no notice of this; she imagined it just the natural change in her life because she was past fifty.

It would not be long now before the ship was launched from the slip, and Joseph was her master.

When he returned in the late spring of 1863 he was startled at the change in her that none but himself could perceive. There were no silvered hairs, no lines, but a general appearance of frailty as though the strength in her had departed; her skin was stretched white over her cheek bones, and the veins showed clearly on her temples. He was frightened and uncertain what to do with her. The thought of possibly losing her he banished from his mind like an evil nightmare, and to make up for it he unwittingly tired her with his love, never leaving her a moment, and thus so much happiness was exhausting to her, pulling her down still further. Instead of calming her and soothing her, his presence acted like a drug that fortifies for the instant, creating an impression of renewed vigour and strength, but leaves its patient weaker than before.

She gave herself to the enjoyment of Joseph with every ounce of power left to her. He enveloped her with his love and devotion until she became dazed and overwrought: it was too strong for her, but she had arrived at the state when she could no longer exist without it. He was at Plyn for some time now, until he had passed his examination at Plymouth, after which he hoped to

The Janet Coombe *was to be carvel-built with a square stern, 97 feet long, her main breadth 22 feet, a little over 12 feet deep, rigged as a two-masted top-sail schooner.*

take command of the new ship to be launched in the summer. The strain of these weeks was almost more than Janet could bear, and when he set off for Plymouth to sit for his examination she waited in a fever for his return. They passed the days in silent agony until the result should be known to them.

At last one morning there arrived an important-looking document, and Joseph made straight to Janet's side so that they should see it together. They unfolded the stiff parchment, stamped with the red seal of the Board of Trade.

'WHEREAS it has been reported to us that you have been found duly qualified to fulfil the duties of Master in the Merchant Service, we do hereby in pursuance of the Merchant Shipping Act 1854 grant you this Certificate of Competency. Given under the Seal of the Board of Trade this ninth day of August 1863.'

Janet held out her arms to him with a cry – he had passed. Joseph, her son, not yet twenty-nine, was a Master in the Merchant Service, the equal of middle-aged men like Captain Collins. There were great rejoicings that day at Ivy House. Janet seated at the head of the table with Joseph on her right hand, and gathered about her the grown-up sons and daughters, and her grandchildren, Samuel's two daughters and his young son, and Herbert's little boy. The next event would be the launching of the ship. Thomas and his sons, including Joseph, held a private consultation when Janet was not present, to decide the all-important matter of the ship's figurehead.

They agreed that it must be taken after Janet herself, but it seemed there was no one in Plyn who was skilled enough to undertake such a task. So a well-known carver in Bristol was commissioned to build the figurehead, and a likeness of Janet as a young woman was sent to him.

The father and his sons rejoiced in their secret, for Janet would know nothing of it until the day of the launching, as the figurehead would be bolted on to the ship's head the evening before.

The last weeks in August had come, the last nails were driven into the planks. The decks were laid and the hull painted. Her masts would be stepped when she was in the water, and there she would be rigged and fitted out for sea.

The *Janet Coombe* was ready to be launched. Her two years of waiting were over, and as the great black ship lay on the slip biding for the high spring tides, it seemed as if her very timbers called for the first embrace of the sea which she would never leave again.

The evening of 1 September was arranged for the launching, just before sunset, when the tide was at its highest. All Plyn was in a fever of excitement, because with the launching of a new ship everybody automatically took a half-holiday, and this ship was to bear the name of Coombe itself.

The evening before, a Sunday, all the family were assembled in the parlour. The weather was warm, and Janet, who was overtired with the preparations, and scarce able to realise that the great day would dawn tomorrow, sat in her chair before the open window, while the cool air played on her face. She would have climbed the hill to the Castle ruins if she had had the strength, but she was too weary. She lay back in her chair, looking down upon the harbour, and let her thoughts wander as they willed.

It seemed to her that in all her life this was the moment for which she had waited. Two other moments only would perhaps equal it. The night on the boat from Plymouth, and the morning she first held Joseph in her arms. But tomorrow her ship, built because of her, would be claimed by the sea, and she would step upon its decks and give her blessing. Life would hold no more for her than the beauty of that moment. Dusk was creeping over Plyn, over the quiet town and the sleeping harbour. Behind, cloaked in shadows, were the hills and the valleys that she loved so well. A supreme feeling of peace and contentment came upon her, she was filled with a love of all things, of people and of places, of Thomas her husband, of her children, and Joseph beyond them all.

From the parlour came the strains of the harmonium. The family were grouped round Mary as they had done for so many years, to sing the Sunday hymn. As the night descended and the stars shone upon Janet's uplifted face, her children opened their voices to their God. 'Abide with me! fast falls the eventide; the darkness deepens; Lord with me abide! When other helpers fail, and comforts flee, Help of the helpless. O abide with me. Swift to its close ebbs out life's little day; Earth's joys grow dim, its glories pass away; change and decay in all around I see; O Thou who changest not, abide with me!'

As Janet listened, sweet and clear above the voices of the others was that of Joseph – 'Abide with me.'

It was close to sunset, and the tide had made its highest mark. The red light of the sky glittered upon the houses, and the parting smile of the sun lingered upon the water. All Plyn was gathered about the slip to watch the ship plunge into the sea. The yard was decorated with flags, and thronged with folk. A chair had been brought for Janet, and she was seated upon it, her hand on Joseph's arm. Her eyes were upon the figurehead of the ship. It was Janet herself, Janet with her dark hair and eyes and her firm chin; dressed in white with her hand at her breast.

The figurehead, Jane Slade herself. She still rests beneath my old bedroom window at Ferryside, where I wrote The Loving Spirit*: 'Placed against the beam is the figurehead of a ship. She leans beyond them all, a little white figure with her hands at her breast, her chin in the air, her eyes gazing towards the sea.*

'High above the clustered houses and the grey harbour waters of Plyn, the loving spirit smiles and is free.'

As she looked on it for the first time her heart throbbed in her bosom and her limbs trembled. This was herself, this was she fulfilling her dream, placed there in the bows of the vessel which bore her name. She forgot everything but that her moment had come, the moment when she would become part of a ship – part of the sea for ever. Mist came into her eyes. She saw nothing of Plyn, nothing of the people about her – only the ship hovering on the brink of the slip waiting for the plunge.

She heard none of the cheers; in her ears were the call of the wind and the cry of the waves. Beyond the hill the sun glimmered for an instant – a ball of fire. A great shout arose from the people: 'There she goes!' The harbour rang with their cries and the mighty crash as the vessel struck the water. At the sound a shudder passed through Janet's body and she opened her arms. Her eyes were filled with a great beauty, like the light of a star, and her soul passed away into the breathing, living ship. Janet Coombe was dead.

February 23rd, 1931. 'Worked hard all the morning, and then caught the 4 o'clock train to London. Daddy and Mummy away for a week. By the way, my book came out today.'

So . . . I had been launched, just as the schooner *Jane Slade* had been launched by her namesake in the last century. How long I would remain afloat depended upon the rocks and shoals, fair weather or foul, that I might find in the seas ahead.

I know that no person will ever get into my blood as a place can, as Cornwall does. People and things pass away but not places.

VESTAVIA HILLS LIBRARY
Vestavia Hills, Alabama

CHAPTER THREE

OLD UNHAPPY, FAR-OFF THINGS

~

'Oh yes, they're queer folks in these parts: but wonderful the more you know 'em,' said Dr Carfax to his companion Monsieur Ledru.

'They strike me as very frank and polite: much like, strangely like the folk of my native Brittany.'

'Polite, yes,' agreed the Cornishman. 'But frank? Well, yes again, when you get to it: but you have to go deep for that stratum, devilish deep – down to "old, unhappy, far-off things," as Wordsworth put it. We are an ancient race, sir: frank and joyous among ourselves, and especially joyous and childish with our own children, but bred in-and-in and secretive.'

Perhaps, like Monsieur Ledru in *Castle Dor*, the feeling of empathy I have with the Cornish people has its roots in my ancestry. For among my forebears, including my great grand-father, were men who were master Breton glass-blowers. They were humble, bourgeois glass-blowers, not at all the aristocratic family that my father and grandfather had thought. They thought that the so-called Busson du Mauriers were connected with a Château Maurier near LeMans, but when I researched the family for my book *The Glass-blowers*, I was delighted to discover that the Bussons had been humble people. Robert, the one who had come to England, called himself Busson-du Maurier because the farmhouse they lived in was called Le Maurier!

Today, as a Cornish resident with Breton forebears, I like to think that the two races, facing an Atlantic seaboard blown by identical gales, washed by the same driving mists, share a common ancestry.

Naturally the sea itself has helped form the Cornish character. Their ancestors were probably immigrant merchants from Mediterranean lands, who sailed the seas in search of riches, and came upon Cornwall by luck or accident. As represented in mythology, the sea is a symbol of the uncertainties of fate. 'You will embark on a fair sea, and at times there will be fair weather and foul,' said the priest on my wedding day at Lanteglos church.

Dozmare Pool. Legends and myths lie deep in the Cornish psyche. This was where Bedivere threw the sword Excalibur, and a thrice-waving hand fastened upon its hilt and then withdrew to unplumbed depths. Once a whisper of a breeze ripples the surface the colour changes and little wavelets splash the shore – then we look for the rising hand to break the surface, reaching for Excalibur.

'Never lose courage. Safe harbour awaits you both in the end.' The imagery was so typical of a Cornishman responsible for the souls of a village whose people depended for centuries on the sea.

Two years earlier, during the wintery January of 1930 – rain, sleet, wind, hail, *and* snow – when I was labouring over Part IV of *The Loving Spirit* and having terrible doubts about the novel as a whole, I was interrupted by great excitement in the harbour. Rockets went off and the lifeboat was called out. The ferryman told me there was a ship in distress off Cannis Rock by Pridmouth. The following day I went to investigate; the entry in my diary reads: 'The day was fine, and after working like one possessed through the morning I crossed the ferry after lunch and walked to Pridmouth. There she was, sure enough, right in the bay on the rocks, the sea breaking against her, and already her iron bottom torn open. I was told the crew had all got off safely. The wood cast

Left: *'When I came to the cove I could see the ship at once, lying offshore with her bows pointed towards the cliffs.'* Rebecca.

Below: *The remains of the disaster may still be seen down on Pridmouth beach.*

on the shore. Even a magazine lying in a pool. People like busy flies on the beach scavenging.' The sight would remain in memory. Not for *The Loving Spirit* but for another book, *Rebecca*, many years later, the seed as yet unsown.

The Cornish fisherman confronts almost daily the uncertainties of the elements, the wilfulness of Fortune with faith and skills accumulated over centuries of experience. That many a fisherman has been drowned and his boat smashed is due, not to ignorance but to the daring and courage flowing in his blood. Wise in the weather, he knows that when the wind backs with the changing of the tide there could be increase in wind and sea, and the smallest miscalculation in the timing of his return to harbour might spell danger, even disaster; but the desire to bring home a full catch and beat the weather will win over prudence every time. Down the years the heroic uncertainties of his ancient trade came to permeate the life of the coastal community, drawing men, women and children into an activity central to their lives.

Another Frenchman, one Alphonse Esquiros who ventured to Cornwall in the nineteenth century, was impressed by the stoicism of the Cornish in the face of great hardship and poverty, but he sought in vain for the scenes of domestic joy and happiness so sweetly described by English poets. The peasants, he found, spoke little, and it was difficult to discover the reason for this silence which at times resembled coldness. Was it indifference to their

'Best of all is the sea itself, with never a sight o' land for days, an' the big waves breakin' astern of you. Wind like a slap on your cheek, an' a sting from the rain.' Joseph Coombe in The Loving Spirit.

Helford village. The fisherman re-enacts the most ancient confrontation between man and his environment.

mode of life? Was it resignation, or that species of tacit contentment which the consciousness of a strict duty accomplished imparted to a man?

In truth it was none of these. The reserve which Monsieur Esquiros observed in the Cornish character was something sturdier, more deep-rooted, a self-sufficiency bred in the bone through centuries of independence and being largely his own master, with a natural scepticism and suspicion of the stranger who asked questions.

Take the tinners, they were at work amongst the rocks and furze of Cornwall back in the Bronze Age, some 1800 years BC, though it was not until the fifteenth century AD that they began to mine beneath the surface. The tinners became an essential part of Cornwall – hunters, seekers – spending themselves in the unending quest for 'treasure' underground. They were a race of individual-ists, making their own terms wherever they streamed or dug for tin, beset by no ring of employers as in other industries. They had a single-minded preference for an ancient occupation that entailed great courage and endurance. And it was their individualism, as much as their own customs and pastimes (such as cock-fighting, wrestling, and hurling, which may sometimes have led to excess,

'No trees here, save one or two that stretched bare branches to the four winds, bent and twisted from centuries of storm, and so black were they by time and tempest that, even if spring did breathe on such a place, no buds would dare to come to leaf for fear the late frost should kill them.' Jamaica Inn. *Tinners like these, below, pausing for their bait, worked amongst the rocks and furze for centuries.*

drunkenness and bloody fights), that made them feared and frowned upon by outsiders.

In the mid-nineteenth century, tin and copper mining boomed in Cornwall, in tune with the advancements in engineering, transport and trade of the Industrial Revolution, and the county became the single largest copper-producing district in the world, responsible for two-thirds of the entire world-wide supply. The boom peaked in the 1860s; copper had been found in Lake Victoria, tin in Malaysia. Foreign competition pricked the bubble, and before the end of the century one third of the mining population of Cornwall had taken their skills to other continents.

The collapse of the industry meant terrible destitution for some. From this period come stories of the tinners as a race of violent men who would stop at nothing, waylay travellers by night and beat them senseless, raid farms, set wrecking parties upon the cliffs with lanterns to lure ships to their doom and plunder them. Such stories were founded on a reality of near starvation.

Many tinners who stayed after the collapse of their industry turned to china-clay, now Cornwall's greatest industry, its mines stretching across a high plateau encompassing White Moor and Hensbarrow Downs, outwards to Luxulyan and St Austell, west to Goss Moor and Indian Queens. Incredibly there are people today who object to the 'scars' that the clay industry has left upon the landscape. I think that the huge spoil-heaps, with their attendant lakes, are absolutely beautiful and get livid when people suggest sowing grass seeds on them. At one stage, there was even a suggestion of building a ski slope there to attract the tourists! (an

Ruins of a copper mine between Treesmill and Colwith. Cornwall was the single largest copper-producing district in the world in the mid-19th Century.

In The Loving Spirit, *Janet Coombe describes the changes that clay brought to Fowey: 'Rough jetties were built where the river and harbour meet . . . Now the harbour was a forest of masts, awaiting their turn at the jetty. The people were delighted with the growth of the town – trade would make them prosperous and rich. Only the old folk grumbled . . . "What be us wantin' with ships an' clay?"'*

Clay mines. Theirs is a strange, almost fantastic beauty . . . like another world.

enterprise described in my novel, *Rule Britannia*.) No, theirs is a strange, almost fantastic beauty; if you go up there it is like another world. Today the clay miners are specialists, brought up to clay from birth, second and third generation, and have the same sense of solidarity as the tinners before them.

Of course I did not know Fowey before the advent of the clay industry. Then the harbour had often been empty save for the old fishing luggers belonging to the folk of Polruan. The men would come back from their fishing or down from their work in the fields, lean over the wall by the slip of Slade's yard, and gossip over their pipes, the nets spread out to dry on the cobbled stones, and naught to watch save the gulls diving for fish in the water, and the smoke curling from their cottage chimneys, with the womenfolk at their doors.

Like the Irish, the Cornish are great raconteurs, and the stories which hold them are invariably connected with sea adventures and smuggling, tales which put imagination to flight and exercise the

For some unable to find work after the boom years, smuggling provided welcome relief from great hardship – men like the 'dirty little blackguard from Redruth' in Jamaica Inn. *Emerging 'from the black earth where he had once entombed himself', he had 'taken to the road as tinker, pedlar, bagman', and lately wrecker.*

dramatic genius that all Cornishmen inherit.

Smuggling came easy to a people who had deployed themselves in piracy during the fifteenth and sixteenth centuries – a legacy of the 100 Years' War when the Cornish provided transport ships to carry Plantagenet armies across the Channel. The owners of these ships found it profitable to attack and board a French vessel, subdue her crew, loot her contents and either sink her or bring her home as a prize. Following the end of the War, the taste remained, eventually to be replaced by smuggling. A reconstructed navy kept foreigners at bay and the vessels that had formerly harassed the French and Spanish coasts slipped into foreign ports on a new, more friendly basis, in search of contraband.

The hey-day of smuggling occurred during the nineteenth century when the Industrial Revolution was upsetting the old tenor of life, fortunes were being made or lost in tin and copper, and society was changing into the 'haves' and 'have-nots'.

Although not all smugglers were needy, smuggling was at root the product of severe economic conditions – the exhaustion of tin seams, fluctuating prices, even the seasonal patterns of fishing. The transgression of the law which it undoubtedly involved, was justified in many a Cornishman's mind by a deeper sense of justice than society's which condemned him to hardship and poverty. You could be a smuggler and yet an honest man in all your dealings; smuggling – or fair-trading, as it was called – smacked of the heroic, and tales of smuggling took their place among the myths

The tinners were a race of individualists, but a third of the mining population had left before the end of the 19th Century.

Smugglers could pull into any one of the hundreds of suitable inlets round the Cornish coast, with their once topical names whose origins are long-forgotten: Bessy's and Stackhouse Cove, Brandy Cove and Lucky Hole.

and legends which lie deep in the Cornish psyche.

But if smuggling was largely the result of poverty, it also appealed to the better off as an extremely profitable business. Quite simply, everybody benefited from smuggling. The tinner down on his luck, the Squire who liked his brandy, the Squire's lady who dressed in lace, even the vicar of the parish – often a relation of the Squire – each participated in his own fashion, and the necessity of sharing hazards made a link between all parties.

Luggers with a thousand yards of canvas in their mainsail and a fifty to 250-ton capacity, could cross the channel in eight hours. A cargo bought for £1,500 in France could be sold in England for £3,000. A boat would pull into any one of the hundreds of suitable inlets round the Cornish coast and then be stored – not necessarily in the inevitable cave of romance and legend but often in the homes or storerooms of obliging persons nearby, frequently merchants who had access to waggons, or neighbouring farmers, or even the local Squire with suitable cellars. Then the contraband would be moved across country often at night in waggons led by horses with muffled hoofs, and it might be secreted away by tinners in sealed-up seams on the lonely moors before final dispersal.

The practice of wrecking was far less widespread. Wrecking was an organised version of scavenging which occurred spontaneously as in the case of the disaster I witnessed at Cannis Rock. But the strange frenzy that sometimes overtook part of the community when it heard that a ship had foundered was a far cry from the savage exploits of organised bands of wreckers, who would lure a ship onto the rocks, trawl the sea of its bounty, and even drown survivors of the wreck as they swam ashore.

Smuggled goods were often stored in the cottages of obliging persons living near the coast. There was widespread acceptance of 'fair-trading' as it was called: 'Smuggling was dangerous; it was fraught with dishonesty; it was forbidden strictly by the law of the land; but was it evil? Mary could not decide.' Jamaica Inn

The mist began to lift very slowly, disclosing the narrow outline of the bay. Rocks became more prominent, and the cliffs took on solidity. The expanse of water widened, opening from a gulf to a bare line of shore that stretched away interminably. To the right in the distance, where the highest part of the cliffs sloped to the sea, Mary made out a faint pin-prick of light. At first she thought it a star, piercing the last curtain of dissolving mist, but reason told her that no star was white, nor ever swayed with the wind on the surface of a cliff. She watched it intently, and it moved again; it was like a small white eye in the darkness. It danced and curtseyed, storm-tossed, as though kindled and carried by the wind itself, a living flare that would not be blown. The group of men on the shingle below heeded it not; their eyes were turned to the dark sea beyond the breakers.

And suddenly Mary was aware of the reason for their indifference, and the small white eye that had seemed at first a thing of friendliness and comfort, winking bravely along in the wild night, became a symbol of horror.

The star was a false light placed there by her uncle and his companions. The pin-prick gleam was evil now, and the curtsy to the wind became a mockery. In her imagination the light burnt fiercer, extending its beam to dominate the cliff, and the colour was white no more, but old and yellow like a scab. Someone watched by the light so that it should not be extinguished. She saw a dark figure pass in front of it, obscuring the gleam for a moment, and then it burnt clear again. The figure became a blot against the grey face of the cliff, moving quickly in the direction of the shore. Whoever it was climbed down the slope to his companions on the shingle. His action was hurried, as though time pressed him, and he was careless in the manner of his coming, for the loose earth and stones slid away from under him, scattering down on to the beach below. The sound startled the men beneath, and for the first time since Mary had watched them they withdrew their attention from the incoming tide and looked up to him. Mary saw him put his hands to his mouth and shout, but his words were caught up in the wind and did not come to her. They reached the little group of men waiting on the shingle, who broke up at once in some excitement, some of them starting half-way up the cliff to meet him; but when he shouted again and pointed to the sea, they ran down towards the breakers, their stealth and silence gone for the moment, the sound of their footsteps heavy on the shingle, their voices topping one another above the crash of the sea. Then one of them – her uncle it was; she recognised his great loping stride and massive shoulders – held up his hand for silence; and they waited, all of them, standing upon the shingle with the

Uncle Joss: 'I've killed men with my own hands, trampled them underwater, beaten them with rocks and stones; and I've never thought no more about it; I've slept in my bed like a child . . . There was a woman once, Mary, she was clinging to a raft, and she had a child in her arms . . . She cried out to me to help her, Mary, and I smashed her face in with a stone.'

waves breaking beyond their feet; spread out in a thin line they were, like crows, their black forms outlined against the white beach. Mary watched with them; and out of the mist and darkness came another pin-prick of light in answer to the first. This new light did not dance and waver as the one on the cliff had done; it dipped low and was hidden, like a traveller weary of his burden, and then it would rise again, pointing high to the sky, a hand flung into the night in a last and desperate attempt to break through the wall of mist that hitherto had defied penetration. The new light drew nearer to the first. The one compelled the other. Soon they would emerge and become two white eyes in the darkness. And still the men crouched motionless upon the narrow strand, waiting for the lights to close with one another.

The second light dipped again; and now Mary could see the shadowed outline of a hull, the black spars like fingers spreading above it, while a white surging sea combed beneath the hull, and hissed, and withdrew again. Closer drew the mast-light to the flare upon the cliff, fascinated and held, like a moth coming to a candle.

Mary could bear no more. She scrambled to her feet and ran down upon the beach, shouting and crying, waving her hands above her head, pitting her voice against the wind and the sea, which tossed it back to her in

mockery. Someone caught hold of her and forced her down upon the beach. Hands stifled her. She was trodden upon and kicked. Her cries died away, smothered by the coarse sacking that choked her, and her arms were dragged behind her back and knotted together, the rough cord searing her flesh.

They left her then, with her face in the shingle, the breakers sweeping towards her not twenty yards away; and as she lay there helpless, the breath knocked from her and her scream of warning strangled in her throat, she heard the cry that had been hers become the cry of others, and fill the air with sound. The cry rose above the searing smash of the sea, and was seized and carried by the wind itself; and with the cry came the tearing splinter of wood, the horrible impact of a massive live thing finding resistance, the shuddering groan of twisting, breaking timber.

Drawn by a magnet, the sea hissed away from the strand, and a breaker, running high above its fellows, flung itself with a crash of thunder upon the

'The cry rose above the searing smash of the sea . . . and with the cry came the tearing splinter of wood, the horrible impact of a massive live thing finding resistance, the shuddering groan of twisting, breaking timber.' Jamaica Inn

lurching ship. Mary saw the black mass that had been a vessel roll slowly upon its side, like a great flat turtle; the masts and spars were threads of cotton, crumpled and fallen. Clinging to the slippery, sloping surface of the turtle were little black dots that would not be thrown; that stuck themselves fast to the splintering wood like limpets; and, when the heaving, shuddering mass beneath them broke monstrously in two, cleaving the air, they fell one by one into the white tongues of the sea, little black dots without life or substance.

A deadly sickness came upon Mary, and she closed her eyes, her face pressed into the shingle. The silence and the stealth were gone; the men who had waited during the cold hours waited no more. They ran like madmen hither and thither upon the beach, yelling and screaming, demented and inhuman. They waded waist-deep into the breakers, careless of danger, all caution spent; snatching at the bobbing, sodden wreckage borne in on the surging tide.

They were animals, fighting and snarling over lengths of splintered wood; they stripped, some of them, and ran naked in the cold December night, the better to fight their way into the sea and plunge their hands amongst the spoil that the breakers tossed to them. They chattered and squabbled like monkeys, tearing things from one another; and one of them kindled a fire in the corner by the cliff, the flame burning strong and fierce in spite of the mizzling rain. The spoils of the sea were dragged up the beach and heaped beside it. The fire cast a ghastly light upon the beach, throwing a yellow brightness that had been black before, and casting long shadows down the beach where the men ran backwards and forwards, industrious and horrible.

'And then Joss Merlyn himself lifted his great head and sniffed the air, turning about him as he stood, watching the clear contours of the cliffs as the darkness slipped away.'

When the first body was washed ashore, mercifully spent and gone, they clustered around it, diving amongst the remains with questing, groping hands, picking it clean as a bone; and, when they had stripped it bare, tearing even at the smashed fingers in search of rings, they abandoned it again, leaving it to loll upon its back in the scum where the tide had been.

Whatever had been the practice hitherto, there was no method in their work tonight. They robbed haphazard, each man for himself; crazy they were and drunk, amazed with this success they had not planned – dogs snapping at the heel of their master whose venture had proved a triumph, whose power this was, whose glory. They followed him where he ran naked amongst the breakers, the water streaming from the hair on his body, a giant above them all.

The tide turned, the water receded, and a new chill came upon the air. The light that swung above them on the cliff, still dancing in the wind, like an old mocking man whose joke has long been played, turned pallid now and dim. A grey colour came upon the water and was answered by the sky. At first the men did not notice the change; they were delirious still, intent upon their prey. And then Joss Merlyn himself lifted his great head and sniffed the air, turning about him as he stood, watching the clear contour of the cliffs as the darkness slipped away; and he shouted suddenly, calling the men to silence, pointing to the sky that was leaden now, and pale.

They hesistated, glancing once more at the wreckage that surged and fell in the trough of the sea, unclaimed as yet and waiting to be salved; and then they turned with one accord and began to run up the beach towards the entrance of the gully, silent once more, without words or gesture, their faces grey and scared in the broadening light. They had outstayed their time. Success had made them careless. The dawn had broken upon them unawares, and by lingering overlong they had risked the accusation which daylight would bring to them. The world was waking up around them: night, that had been their ally, covered them no more.

JAMAICA INN

'They turned with one accord and began to run up the beach towards the entrance of the gully . . . their faces grey and scared in the broadening light.'

I owe my first sight of Jamaica Inn to a suggestion by Sir Arthur Quiller-Couch about a year after I had completed *The Loving Spirit*. Son of a Cornish doctor, Sir Arthur, or 'Q' as he was known to countless of his readers, was an important literary figure. Perhaps most famous as editor of the first *Oxford Book of English Verse*, he had been knighted in 1910 and two years later had been appointed to the chair of English at Cambridge. Our friendship began when I was invited one Sunday to tea.

I remember that I was careful to wash and change out of my usual ragged attire before making my way to his home, The Haven, in Fowey. I had no desire to cut a shabby figure before the great man and his family. I recorded the occasion in my diary: 'Lady Q, their daughter Foy, an aunt, an old friend Mr Phelps and a retired parson were there, and we sat down to a big tea in the dining room. I thoroughly enjoyed myself, and liked Foy immensely. She loves the sea just as I do, and there was plenty to talk about.

I stayed on after the others had gone. They belong here, if anyone does, and are Cornish to the last drop of their blood.'

Soon Sunday suppers with the Quiller-Couches became routine, a happy relaxation after the week's work. They were so friendly and sympathetic always, their quiet humour a real tonic. Then in November 1930, Q suggested that Foy and I should take a couple of horses and make an expedition to Bodmin Moor, putting up at the wayside hostelry, Jamaica Inn.

Bodmin is the greatest and wildest stretch of moorland in Cornwall. Rough tracks off the main A30, which cuts across its centre, lead to isolated farms whose inhabitants once hardly ventured forth except to market, owners of sheep and cattle who

'No trees, no lanes, no cluster of cottages or hamlet, but mile upon mile of bleak moorland, dark and untraversed, rolling like a desert land to some unseen horizon . . . They would be born of strange stock who slept with this earth as pillow, beneath this black sky. They would have something of the Devil left in them still.'

Left: *I thought of the inn as it had been before it became the Temperance House I visited in 1930, a bar where the little parlour was, the drinking deep and long, fights breaking out, the sound of oaths, men falling.*

'Mary Yellan found herself northward bound from Helston in the creaking, swaying coach, through Truro town . . . the people at the doors smiling and waving as the coach rattled past. But when Truro lay behind in the valley the sky came overcast . . .'

lived on their own produce and cut moorland turf for fuel. The wanderer who is fond of solitude can wander anywhere on either side of the main road and lose himself forthwith, turning, after he has walked barely half a mile in open country, to see no sign of human habitation, nothing but bare brown moor as far as the eye can reach, rising in the distance to frowning tors and craggy rocks that might give shelter if a rain-shower came, but little comfort from the wind which seeks out clefts and crannies even if the day is still.

Like Mary Yellan who, in the novel, comes to Bodmin Moor from the tranquil hills and valleys of Helford, I came unprepared for its dark, diabolic beauty. People say that my fictional characters seem to emerge from the places where my stories are set, and certainly when I first set eyes on the old, granite-faced Inn itself it made me think that there was a story there, peopled with moorland folk in strange harmony with their background.

It was a cold grey day in late November. The weather had changed overnight, when a backing wind brought a granite sky and a mizzling rain

'It was a silent, desolate country though, vast and untouched by human hand; on the high tours the slabs of stone leant against one another in strange shapes and forms, massive sentinels who had stood there since the hand of God first fashioned them.'

'It was a scrubby land, without hedgerow or meadow; a country of stones, black heather, and stunted broom.'

with it, and although it was now only a little after two o'clock in the afternoon the pallor of a winter evening seemed to have closed upon the hills, cloaking them in mist. It would be dark by four. The air was clammy cold, and for all the tightly closed windows it penetrated the interior of the coach. The leather seats felt damp to the hands, and there must have been a small crack in the roof, because now and again little drips of rain fell softly through, smudging the leather and leaving a dark-blue stain like a splodge of ink. The wind came in gusts, at times shaking the coach as it travelled round the bend of the road, and in the exposed places on the high ground it blew with such force that the whole body of the coach trembled and swayed, rocking between the high wheels like a drunken man.

The driver, muffled in a greatcoat to his ears, bent almost double in his seat in a faint endeavour to gain shelter from his own shoulders, while the dispirited horses plodded sullenly to his command, too broken by the wind and the rain to feel the whip that now and again cracked above their heads, while it swung between the numb fingers of the driver. . .

The country was alien to her, which was a defeat in itself. As she peered through the misty window of the coach she looked out upon a different world from the one she had known only a day's journey back. How remote now and hidden perhaps for ever were the shining waters of Helford, the green hills and the sloping valleys, the white cluster of cottages at the water's edge! It was a gentle rain that fell at Helford, a rain that pattered in the many trees and lost itself in the lush grass, formed into the brooks and rivulets that emptied into the broad river, sank into the grateful soil which gave back flowers in payment.

This was a lashing, pitiless rain that stung the windows of the coach, and it soaked into a hard and barren soil. No trees here, save one or two that stretched bare branches to the four winds, bent and twisted from centuries of storm, and so black were they by time and tempest that, even if spring did breathe on such a place, no buds would dare to come to leaf for fear the late frost should kill them. It was a scrubby land, without hedgerow or meadow; a country of stones, black heather, and stunted broom.

There would never be a gentle season here, thought Mary; either grim winter as it was today, or else the dry and parching heat of mid-summer, with never a valley to give shade or shelter, but grass that turned yellow-brown before May was passed. The country had gone grey with the weather. Even the people on the road and in the villages changed in harmony with their background. . .

It was dark in the coach now, for the torch gave forth a sickly yellow glare, and the draught from the crack in the roof sent the flame wandering hither and thither, to the danger of the leather, and Mary thought it best to extinguish it. She sat huddled in her corner, swaying from side to side as the coach was shaken, and it seemed to her that never before had she known there was malevolence in solitude. The very coach, which all the day had rocked her like a cradle, now held a note of menace in its creaks and groans. The wind tore at the roof, and the showers of rain, increasing in violence now there was no shelter from the hills, spat against the windows with new venom. On either side of the road the country stretched interminably into space. No trees, no lanes, no cluster of cottages or hamlet, but mile upon mile of bleak moorland, dark and untraversed, rolling like a desert land to some unseen horizon. No human being could live in this wasted country, thought Mary, and remain like other people; the very children would be born twisted, like the blackened shrubs of broom, bent by the force of a wind that never ceased, blow as it would from east and west, from north and south. Their minds would be twisted, too, their thoughts evil, dwelling as they must

'No human being could live in this wasted country, thought Mary, and remain like other people; the very children would be born twisted.'

amidst marshland and granite, harsh heather and crumbling stone.

They would be born of strange stock who slept with this earth as a pillow, beneath this black sky. They would have something of the Devil left in them still. On wound the road across the dark and silent land, with never a light to waver for an instant as a message of hope to the traveller within the coach. Perhaps there was no habitation in all the long one-and-twenty miles that stretched between the two towns of Bodmin and Launceston; perhaps there was not even a poor shepherd's hut on the desolate highway; nothing but the one grim landmark that was Jamaica Inn.

Mary lost count of time and space; the miles might have been a hundred and the hour midnight for all she knew. She began to cling to the safety of the coach; at least it had some remnant of familiarity. She had known it since the early morning, and that was long ago. However great a nightmare was this eternal drive, there were at least the four close walls to protect her, the shabby leaking roof, and, within calling distance, the comfortable presence of the driver. At last it seemed to her that he was driving his horses to an even greater speed; she heard him shout to them; the cry of his voice blown past her window on the wind.

She lifted the sash and looked out. She was met with a blast of wind and rain that blinded her for the moment, and then, shaking clear her hair and pushing it from her eyes, she saw that the coach was topping the breast of a hill at a furious gallop, while on either side of the road was rough moorland, looming ink-black in the mist and rain.

Ahead of her, on the crest, and to the left, was some sort of a building, standing back from the road. She could see tall chimneys, murky dim in the darkness. There was no other house, no other cottage. If this was Jamaica, it stood alone in glory, four-square to the winds. Mary gathered her cloak around her and fastened the clasp. The horses had been pulled to a standstill and stood sweating under the rain, the steam coming from them in a cloud.

The driver climbed down from his seat, pulling her box down with him.

'If this was Jamaica, it stood alone in glory, four-square to the winds.'

He seemed hurried, and he kept glancing over his shoulder towards the house.

'Here you are,' he said; 'across the yard there yonder. If you hammer on the door they'll let you in. I must be getting on or I'll not reach Launceston tonight.' In a moment he was up on his seat again, and picking up the reins. He shouted at his horses, whipping them in a fever of anxiety. The coach rumbled and shook, and in a moment it was away and down the road, disappearing as though it had never been, lost and swallowed up in the darkness.

Mary stood alone, with the trunk at her feet. She heard a sound of bolts being drawn in the dark house behind her, and the door was flung open. A great figure strode into the yard, swinging a lantern from side to side.

'Who is it?' came the shout. 'What do you want here?'

Mary stepped forward and peered up into the man's face.

The light shone in her eyes, and she could see nothing. He swung the lantern to and fro before her, and suddenly he laughed and told hold of her arm, pulling her roughly inside the porch.

'Oh, it's you, is it?' he said. 'So you've come to us after all? I'm your uncle, Joss Merlyn, and I bid you welcome to Jamaica Inn.' He drew her into the shelter of the house, laughing again, and shut the door, and stood the lantern upon a table in the passage. And they looked upon each other face to face.

Presentiments of evil evoked by the desolate moorland scene are compounded in Mary's mind by the dark and imposing character of Joss, and the sudden arrival of waggons at the Inn in the dead of night. In the pretty fishing village of Helford, when there was talk of smuggling, it was with a wink and a smile of indulgence, as though a pipe of baccy and a bottle of brandy from a ship in Falmouth port was an occasional harmless luxury and not a burden on any person's conscience. But at Jamaica there is precious little smiling or winking, as Mary discovers when she is awakened by a noise coming from the courtyard beneath her window.

Mary Yellan's bedroom window, above the porch, from which she sees the waggons pull up in the yard.

She listened, hearing nothing at first but the thumping of her own heart, but in a few minutes there came another sound, from beneath her room this time – the sound of heavy things being dragged along the stone flags in the passage downstairs, bumping against the walls.

She got out of bed and went to the window, pulling aside an inch of blind. Five waggons were drawn up in the yard outside. Three were covered, each drawn by a pair of horses, and the remaining two were open farm-carts. One of the covered waggons stood directly beneath the porch, and the horses were steaming.

Gathered round the waggons were some of the men who had been drinking in the bar earlier in the evening; the cobbler from Launceston was standing under Mary's window, talking to a horse-dealer; the sailor from Padstow had come to his senses and was patting the head of a horse; the pedlar who had tortured the poor idiot was climbing into one of the open carts and lifting

'They came singly, the people of the moors, crossing the yard swiftly and silently, as though they had no wish to be seen. They lacked substance, in the dim light, and seemed no more than shadows.'

something from the floor. And there were strangers in the yard whom Mary had never seen before. She could see their faces clearly because of the moonlight, the very brightness of which seemed to worry the men, for one of them pointed upwards and shook his head, while his companion shrugged his shoulders, and another man, who had an air of authority about him, waved his arm impatiently, as though urging them to make haste, and the three of them turned at once and passed under the porch into the inn. Meanwhile the heavy dragging sound continued, and Mary could trace the direction of it without difficulty from where she stood. Something was being taken along the passage to the room at the end, the room with the barred windows and the bolted door.

She began to understand. Packages were brought by the waggons and unloaded at Jamaica Inn. They were stored in the locked room. Because the horses were steaming, they had come over a great distance – from the coast perhaps – and as soon as the waggons were unloaded they would take their departure, passing out into the night as swiftly and as silently as they had come.

The men in the yard worked quickly, against time. The contents of one covered waggon were not carried into the inn, but were tranferred to one of the open farm-carts drawn up beside the drinking-well across the yard. The packages seemed to vary in size and description; some were large parcels, some were small, and others were long rolls wrapped round about in straw and paper. When the cart was filled, the driver, a stranger to Mary, climbed into the seat and drove away.

The remaining waggons were unloaded one by one, and the packages were either placed in the open carts and driven out of the yard, or were borne by the men into the house. All was done in silence. Those men who had shouted and sung earlier that night, were now sober and quiet, bent on the business in hand. Even the horses appeared to understand the need for silence, for they stood motionless.

Joss Merlyn came out of the porch, the pedlar at his side. Neither wore coat or hat, in spite of the cold air, and both had sleeves rolled to the elbows.

'Is that the lot?' the landlord called softly, and the driver of the last waggon nodded, and held up his hand. The men began to climb into the carts. Some of those who had come to the inn on foot went with them, saving themselves a mile or two on their long trek home. They did not leave unrewarded; all carried burdens of a sort; boxes strapped over their shoulders, bundles under the arm; while the cobbler from Launceston had not only laden his pony with bursting saddle-bags but had added to his own person as well, being several sizes larger round the waist than when he first arrived.

So the waggons and the carts departed from Jamaica, creaking out of the yard, one after the other in a strange funereal procession, some turning north and some south when they came out on to the high road, until they had all gone, and there was no one left standing in the yard but one man Mary had not seen before, the pedlar, and the landlord of Jamaica Inn himself.

Then they too turned, and went back into the house, and the yard was empty. She heard them go along the passage in the direction of the bar, and

'They say the shouting from Jamaica and the singing can be heard as far down as the farms below Roughtor.'

then their footsteps died away, and a door slammed. . .

She dressed hurriedly, and pulled on her stockings, leaving her shoes where they were, and then, opening the door, she stood and listened for a moment, hearing nothing but the slow choking tick of the clock in the hall.

She crept out into the passage, and came to the stairs. By now she knew that the third step from the top creaked, and so did the last. She trod gently, one hand resting on the banister and the other against the wall to lighten her weight, and so she came to the dim hall by the entrance-door, empty except for one unsteady chair and the shadowed outline of the grandfather clock. Its husky breathing sounded loud beside her ear, and it jarred upon the silence like a living thing. The hall was as black as a pit, and, although she knew she stood alone there, the very solitude was threatening, the closed door to the unused parlour pregnant with suggestion.

The air was fusty and heavy, in strange contrast to the cold stone flags that struck chill to her stockinged feet. As she hesitated, gathering courage to continue, a sudden beam of light shone into the passage that ran at the back of the hall, and she heard voices. The door of the bar must have swung open, and someone came out, for she heard footsteps pass into the kitchen and in a few minutes return again, but whoever it was still left the door of the bar ajar, as the murmur of voices continued and the beam of light remained. Mary was tempted to climb the stairs again to her bedroom and seek safety in sleep, but at the same time there was a demon of curiosity within her that would not be stilled, and this part of her carried her through to the passage beyond, and so to crouch against the wall a few paces only from the door of

Wrecking country: 'Only the gulls and the wild birds haunt the cliffs from Boscastle to Hartland.'

the bar. Her hands and her forehead were wet now with perspiration, and at first she could hear nothing but the loud beating of her heart. The door was open enough for her to see the outline of the hinged bar itself, and the collection of bottles and glasses, while directly in front ran a narrow strip of floor. The splinterd fragments of the glass her uncle had broken still lay where they had fallen, and beside them was a brown stain of ale, spilt by some unsteady hand. The men must be sitting on the benches against the farther wall, for she could not see them; they had fallen to silence, and then suddenly a man's voice rang out, quavering and high, the voice of a stranger.

'No, and no again,' he said. 'I tell you for the final time, I'll not be a party to it. I'll break with you now, and for ever, and put an end to the agreement. That's murder you'd have me do, Mr Merlyn; there's no other name for it – it's common murder.'

The voice was pitched high, trembling on the final note, as though the speaker was carried away by the force of his feelings and had lost command of his tongue. Someone – the landlord himself, no doubt – made reply in a low tone, and Mary could not catch his words, but his speech was broken by a cackle of laughter that she recognised as belonging to the pedlar. The quality of it was unmistakable – insulting and coarse.

He must have hinted a question, for the stranger spoke again swiftly in self-defence. 'Swinging, is it?' he said. 'I've risk swinging before, and I'm not afraid of my neck. No, I'm thinking of my conscience and of Almighty God; and though I'll face any man in a fair fight, and take punishment if need be, when it comes to the killing of innocent folk, and maybe women and children amongst them, that's going straight to hell, Joss Merlyn, and you know it as well as I do.'

Mary heard the scraping of a chair, and the man rise to his feet, but at the same time someone thumped his fist on the table and swore, and her uncle lifted his voice for the first time.

'Not so fast, my friend,' he said, 'not so fast. You're soaked in this business up to your neck, and be damned to your blasted conscience! I tell you there's no going back on it now; it's too late; too late for you and for all of us. I've been doubtful of you from the first, with your gentleman's airs and your clean cuffs, and by God I've proved myself right. Harry, bolt the door over there and put the bar across it.'

There was a sudden scuffle and a cry, and the sound of someone falling, and at the same time the table crashed to the floor, and the door to the yard was slammed. Once more the pedlar laughed, odious and obscene, and he began to whistle one of his songs. 'Shall we tickle him up like Silly Sam?' he said, breaking off in the middle. 'He'd be a little body without his fine clothes. I could do with his watch and chain, too; poor men of the road like myself haven't the money to go buying watches. Tickle him up with the whip, Joss, and let's see the colour of his skin.'

'Shut your mouth, Harry, and do as you're told,' answered the landlord. 'Stand where you are by the door and prick him with your knife if he tries to pass you. Now, look here, Mr lawyer-clerk, or whatever you are in Truro town, you've made a fool of yourself tonight, but you're not going to make a fool of me. You'd like to walk out of the door, wouldn't you, and get on your horse, and be away to Bodmin? Yes, and by nine in the morning, you'd have every magistrate in the country at Jamaica Inn, and a regiment of soldiers into the bargain. That's your fine idea, isn't it?'

Mary could hear the stranger breathe heavily, and he must have been hurt in the scuffle, for when his voice came it was jerky and contracted, as though he were in pain. 'Do your devil's work if you must,' he muttered. 'I can't stop you, and I give you my word I'll not inform against you. But join you I will not, and there's my last word to you both.'

There was a silence, and then Joss Merlyn spoke again. 'Have a care,' he said softly. 'I heard another man say that once, and five minutes later he was treading the air. On the end of a rope it was, my friend, and his big toe missed the floor by half an inch. I asked him if he liked to be so near the ground, but he didn't answer. The rope forced the tongue out of his mouth, and he bit it clean in half. They said afterwards he had taken seven and three-quarter minutes to die.'

Outside in the passage Mary felt her neck and her forehead go clammy with sweat, and her arms and legs were weighted suddenly, as though with lead. Little black specks flickered before her eyes, and with a growing sense of horror she realised that she was probably going to faint.

She had one thought in her mind, and that was to grope her way back to the deserted hall and reach the shadow of the clock; whatever happened she must not fall here and be discovered. Mary backed away from the beam of light, and felt along the wall with her hands. Her knees were shaking now, and she knew that at any moment they would give beneath her. Already a surge of sickness rose inside her, and her head was swimming.

Her uncle's voice came from very far away, as though he spoke with his hands against his mouth. 'Leave me alone with him, Harry,' he said; 'there'll be no more work for you tonight at Jamaica. Take his horse and be off, and cast him loose the other side of Camelford. I'll settle this business by myself.'

Somehow Mary found her way to the hall, and, hardly conscious of what she was doing, she turned the handle of the parlour door and stumbled inside. Then she crumpled in a heap on the floor, her head between her knees.

Now convinced that there is more to Joss's work than smuggling, one afternoon Mary decides to follow her uncle as he makes a sudden departure on foot across the West Moor, behind the Inn.

Her task was a difficult one, and after a few miles she began to realise it. She was forced to keep a good length between them in order to remain unseen, and the landlord walked at such a pace, and took such tremendous strides, that before long Mary saw she would be left behind. Codda Tor was passed, and he turned west now towards the low ground at the foot of Brown Willy, looking, for all his height, like a little black dot against the brown stretch of moor.

The prospect of climbing some thirteen hundred feet came as something of a shock to Mary, and she paused for a moment, and wiped her streaming face. She let down her hair, for greater comfort, and let it blow about her face. Why the landlord of Jamaica Inn thought it necessary to climb the highest point on Bodmin Moor on a December afternoon she could not tell,

'Mary could make out a curious groaning sound like an animal in pain . . . a dark shape swinging gently to and fro. For one nightmare moment she thought it was a gibbet, and a dead man hanging. And then she realised it was the signboard of the inn that swung backwards, forwards, with the slightest breeze.'

but, having come so far, she was determined to have some satisfaction for her pains, and she set off again at a sharper pace.

The ground was now soggy beneath her feet, for here the early frost had thawed and turned to water, and the whole of the low-lying plain before her was soft and yellow from the winter rains. The damp oozed into her shoes with cold and clammy certainty, and the hem of her skirt was bespattered with bog and torn in places. Lifting it up higher, and hitching it round her waist with the ribbon from her hair, Mary plunged on in trail of her uncle, but he had already traversed the worst of the low ground with uncanny quickness born of long custom, and she could just make out his figure amongst the black heather and the great boulders at the foot of Brown Willy. Then he was hidden by a jutting crag of granite, and she saw him no more.

It was impossible to discover the path he had taken across the bog; he had been over and gone in a flash, and Mary followed as best she could, floundering at every step. She was a fool to attempt it, she knew that, but a sort of stubborn stupidity made her continue. Ignorant of the whereabouts of the track that had carried her uncle dry-shod over the bog, Mary had sense enough to make a wide circuit to avoid the treacherous ground, and, by going

'Codda Tor was passed, and he turned west now towards the low ground at the foot of Brown Willy.'

quite two miles in the wrong direction, she was able to cross in comparative safety. She was now hopelessly left, without a prospect of ever finding her uncle again.

Nevertheless she set herself to climb Brown Willy, slipping and stumbling amongst the wet moss and the stones, scrambling up the great peaks of jagged granite that frustrated her at every turn, while now and again a hill sheep, startled by the sound of her, ran out from behind a boulder to gaze at her and stamp his feet. Clouds were bearing up from the west, casting changing shadows on the plains beneath, and the sun went in behind them.

It was very silent on the hills. Once a raven rose up at her feet and screamed; he went away flapping his great black wings, swooping to the earth below with harsh protesting cries.

When Mary reached the summit of the hill the evening clouds were banked high above her head, and the world was grey. The distant horizon was blotted out in the gathering dusk, and thin white mist rose from the moors beneath. Approaching the tor from its steepest and most difficult side, as she had done, she had wasted nearly an hour out of her time, and darkness would soon be upon her. Her escapade had been to little purpose, for as far as her eyes could see there was no living thing within their range.

Joss Merlyn had long vanished; and for all she knew he might not have climbed the tor at all, but skirted its base amongst the rough heather and the smaller stones, and then made his way alone and unobserved, east or west as his business took him, to be swallowed up in the folds of the farther hills.

Mary would never find him now. The best course was to descend the tor by the shortest possible way and in the speediest fashion, otherwise she would be faced with the prospect of a winter's night upon the moors, with dead-black heather for a pillow and no other shelter but frowning crags of granite. She knew herself now for a fool to have ventured so far on a December afternoon, for experience had proved to her that there were no

Joss Merlyn's younger brother, Jem, with whom Mary falls in love, makes his living from horses on the moors: 'Thieving is an awkward thing to prove . . . Well, you've seen for yourself, these moors are alive with wild horses and cattle.'

Brown Willy 'lifting his mighty head in lonely splendour behind her.'

Mary came 'at length to a rough track bearing ahead and slightly to the right. This at any rate had served for a cart's wheels at one time or another.'

long twilights on Bodmin Moor. When darkness came it was swift and sudden, without warning, and an immediate blotting out of the sun. The mists were dangerous too, rising in a cloud from the damp ground and closing in about the marshes like a white barrier.

Discouraged and depressed, and all excitement gone from her, Mary scrambled down the steep face of the tor, one eye on the marshes below and the other for the darkness that threatened to overtake her. Directly below her there was a pool or well, said to be the source of the river Fowey that ran ultimately to the sea, and this must be avoided at all costs, for the ground around was boggy and treacherous and the well itself of an unknown depth.

She bore to her left to avoid it, but by the time she had reached the level of the plain below, with Brown Willy safely descended and lifting his mighty head in lonely splendour behind her, the mist and the darkness had settled on the moors and all sense of direction was now lost to her.

Whatever happened she must keep her head, and not give way to her growing sense of panic. Apart from the mist the evening was fine, and not too cold, and there was no reason why she should not hit upon some track that would lead ultimately to habitation.

There was no danger from the marshes if she kept to the high ground, so, trussing up her skirt again and wrapping her shawl firmly round her shoulders, Mary walked steadily before her, feeling the ground with some care when in doubt, and avoiding those tufts of grass that felt soft and yielding to her feet. That the direction she was taking was unknown to her was obvious in the first few miles, for her way was barred suddenly by a stream that she had not passed on the outward journey. To travel by its side would only lead her once more to the low-lying ground and the marshes, so she plunged through it recklessly soaking herself above the knee. Wet shoes and stockings did not worry her; she counted herself fortunate that the stream had not been deeper, which would have meant swimming for it, and a chilled body into the bargain. The ground now seemed to rise in front of her,

The church at Altarnun whose strange vicar is the rider whom Mary encounters on Bodmin Moor. 'He was different from any man she had seen before. He looked like a bird. Crouched in his seat, with his black cape-coat blown out in the wind, his arms were like wings . . . She felt a sensation of uneasiness.'

which was all to the good, as the going was firm, and she struck boldly across the high downland for what seemed to be an interminable distance, coming at length to a rough track bearing ahead and slightly to the right. This at any rate had served for a cart's wheels at one time or other, and where a cart could go Mary could follow. The worst was past; and now that her real anxiety had gone she felt weak and desperately tired.

Her limbs were heavy, dragging things that scarcely belonged to her, and her eyes felt sunken away back in her head. She plodded on, her chin low and her hands at her side, thinking that the tall grey chimneys of Jamaica Inn would be, for the first time perhaps in their existence, a welcome and consoling sight. The track broadened now, and was crossed in turn by another running left and right, and Mary stood uncertainly for a few moments, wondering which to take. It was then that she heard the sound of a horse, blowing as though he had been ridden hard, coming out of the darkness to the left of her. . .

On the first afternoon following our arrival at Jamaica nearly sixty years ago, Foy and I experienced first-hand the despondency and near-panic that Mary felt. We had set out on horseback with the happy intention of calling on an elderly lady living at Trebartha Hall about five miles east of the Inn.

Surely, we told ourselves, it would be no more than forty minutes' ride at most; and if we stayed to tea then we must make up our minds to skirt the moor on our homeward track, and jog

Mary sets off across the east moor from Jamaica to find Jem's cottage (a walk best undertaken on a fine day with plenty of light). She walks to Rushyford Gate, avoiding Trewartha Marsh where Matthew Merlyn drowned, fords the Withey Brook (right), which 'burbled merrily over the stones', and arrives on Twelve Men's Moor.

back to Jamaica Inn by road. Irresponsible, we trotted off across the moor no later than two o'clock, only to find after an hour or more that we were little nearer to our destination, that tors and boulders inaccessible on horseback, even perhaps on foot, barred our passage. The track leading us on descended to a slippery path that disappeared, while beneath us a battered gate, swinging by the hinges, gave access to a swollen stream. The day, comparatively fine until that moment, darkened, and a black cloud, trailing ribbons, hovered above our heads and burst.

In a moment all was desolation. The ominous stream rushed by with greater swiftness, turning to a torrent. Forcing the horses up a steep incline, to put distance between ourselves and the running water, our heads bent low to our saddles, we plunged onward, seeking escape. A deserted cottage, humped beneath the hill, seemed our only hope – at least it would be temporary refuge until the cloudburst ceased. We rode towards it, dismounted, and led our horses to the rear. The cottage was not only empty but part fallen, with rain driving through the empty windows, and what roof there was had been repaired with corrugated tin, so that the cascading rain sounded like hailstones on its surface. We leant against the fungoid walls and brooded, Trebartha Hall a hundred miles away, Jamaica Inn an equal distance, and all the while the rain fell upon the corrugated roof to echo in a splashing water-butt near by. I had never known greater despondency.

It rained for a full hour, then turned to drizzle and dank fog, by which time our world was murky and we had lost all sense of compass points. Emerging from the ruins my companion, a better horsewoman than I and owner of both our steeds, looked about her and observed, 'There's nothing for it but to get into the saddle,

Joss Merlyn: 'I'm the eldest of three brothers, all of us born under the shadow of Kilmar Tor, away yonder above Twelve Men's Moor.' The ruins of Jem Merlyn's 'small grey cottage on the side of the hill' can be seen at the foot of the moor.

leave our reins loose on their necks, and let them lead us home.'

I was not impressed by her suggestion, for where was home to the horses – thirty miles or more to Fowey, or back across the moors to Jamaica Inn? We mounted once again, darkness and silence all about us, save for that dreary patter on the cottage roof, and somewhere to our right the hissing stream.

The horses, sure-footed even amongst dead heather and loose stones, plodded forward without hesitation, and there was some relief at least to be away from the abandoned cottage and in the open, however desolate, for there had been no warmth within its walls, no memories of hearths glowing with turf fire kindled by owners in the past. Surely whoever lived there before he let it fall to ruins had been sullen and morose, plagued by the Withey Brook that ran somewhere below his door, and in despair went out one night and drowned himself. I suggested this to my fellow-traveller, who was not amused, especially as the horses seemed attracted to the river sound. Gaining higher ground we found ourselves facing a new hazard in the form of what appeared to be a disused railway track, upon which our mounts slithered and stumbled. A railroad in mid-moor. It could not be. Unless we had both gone mad and this was fantasy.

'A line for trolleys,' said my companion, 'leading to a stone-quarry. If the horses take us there they'll break their legs. Better

Kilmar Tor: 'Away to the westward arctic winter fell upon the hills, brought by a jagged cloud shaped like a highwayman's cloak.'

dismount.' Bogs, quarries, brooks, boulders, hell on every side, we led the horses from the slippery track, and then got up on our saddles once again. I remembered an illustration from a book read long ago in childhood, *Sintram, And His Companions*, where a dispirited knight had travelled such a journey with the devil in disguise, who called himself The Little Master. It showed a terrified steed rearing near a precipice. This was to be our fate, and The Little Master would come and claim us.

The horses, bolder now they were free of the trolley-lines, headed steadily forward, straight across the moor, possibly in the direction of those menacing crags that we had seen in early afternoon, pointing dark fingers to the sky, which, we knew very well, lay contrary to any path for home.

It was seven, it was nine, it was midnight – too dark to see our

Take a walk behind Jamaica and, one morning before sunrise, climb Rough Tor and listen to the wind in the stones. These moors have a fascination unlike any other, they are a survival from another age.

watches, and fumbling fingers could not strike damp matches. On, forever on, nothing on all sides but waste and moor.

Suddenly my companion cried, 'They've done it . . . they've done it . . . Isn't that the road?'

Peering into the darkness ahead I saw a break in the rising ground, and a new flatness, and there, not a hundred yards distant, the blessed streaky wetness of the Launceston-Bodmin road, and surprisingly, unbelievably, the gaunt chimneys of Jamaica Inn itself.

'I told you so,' called the expert, 'horses always know the way. They travel by instinct. See, the people from the Inn have come to look for us,' and sure enough there were figures with tossing lanterns wandering to and fro upon the road, and welcoming lamplight shone from the slated porch. In an instant fear was forgotten, danger had never been. It was just eight o'clock, the landlord and his wife had only then begun to think of us, and here was the turf fire for which we had longed, brown and smoky sweet, a supper of eggs and bacon ready to be served with a pot of scalding tea.

The landmarks we had encountered became landmarks in the novel – Trewartha Tor, Hawk's Tor and Kilmar Tor, below which lies the romantic sounding Twelve Men's Moor, teeming with granite boulders and broken trees, splashed about with seeping bogs – indeed, Mary follows the route when later she goes in search of Joss's brother Jem and travels with him to Launceston Fair. They are more easily approached from the east, a steep car-climb from North Hill village and then a brief trek on foot.

Today all is changed at the Inn itself. Coaches, cars, electricity, a bar, dinner of river-trout, baths for the travel-stained instead of the cream-jug of hot water that we were offered. I must take my share of the blame because out of that November expedition long ago came a novel which proved so popular that it passed into the folk-lore of the district.

But if, when you go there, you wonder whether the novel was pure fancy rather than an expression of the spirit of the place as I saw it, take a walk behind Jamaica and, one morning before sunrise, climb Rough Tor and listen to the wind in the stones. These moors have a fascination unlike any other, they are a survival from another age. They were the first things to be created; afterwards came the forests and the valleys and the sea. Nothing has really changed since Mary Yellan walked the moors, climbed the tors, and rested in the low dips beside the springs and streams.

Strange winds blew from nowhere; they crept along the surface of the grass, and the grass shivered; they breathed upon the little pools of rain in the

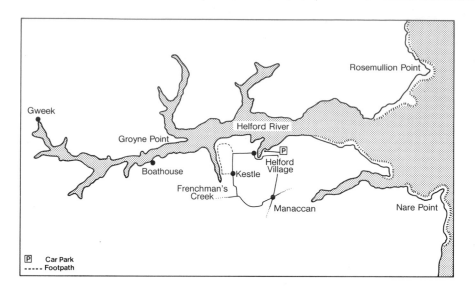

P   Car Park
----- Footpath

The Helford River and Frenchman's Creek. If you leave your car in the car park above Helford there's a wonderful walk down through the village, up the steep track the other side, and thence along the east bank of the Creek itself. Alternatively you can hire a boat at Helford and explore by river, but beware low tide.

hollowed stones, and the pools rippled. Sometimes the wind shouted and cried, and the cry echoed in the crevices, and moaned, and was lost again. There was a silence on the tors that belonged to another age; an age that is past and vanished as though it had never been, an age when man did not exist, but pagan footsteps trod upon the hills. And there was a stillness in the air, and a stranger, older peace, that was not the peace of God.

How remote indeed from the shining waters of the Helford. Here the rain, no longer driving across high barren ground, falls in a mizzle. A sluggish indolence pervades. The stranger, coaxing his

'How remote now and hidden perhaps for ever were the shining waters of Helford, the green hills and the sloping valleys, the white cluster of cottages at the water's edge.'

Helford Village: 'The tripper eats his split and drinks his tea, smiling upon the landscape, knowing nothing of the woman who stood there once, long ago in another summer.' Frenchman's Creek

boat up-river in a sudden windless calm casts anchor with a yawn beside pool or creek, then lolls by the tiller, too idle to row ashore. Peace prevails. The tide ebbs. The gently wooded slopes on either side of him that seemed at first sight to touch the water's edge appear more distant. Mud-banks form beneath them, oozing and soft, or little steep-to beaches of grey slate.

Birds, save for the gulls that piloted him to port, have hitherto been absent. Now they are everywhere. Oyster-catchers (sea-pie to the Cornish) with a quick seeping cry, swoop to the mud-banks in a flash of black and white. Further up-river, where a dead branch from a fallen tree, strung about with sea-weed, overhangs the water, a heron stalks, prinking his way like some grave professor fearing to lose a galosh, then suddenly stands and broods, his wings humped, his head buried in his feathers.

Here I set the only one of my novels that I am prepared to admit is romantic. A woman of means falls in love with a pirate – it sounds almost ridiculous! But there is a reason for the romance – there's a romantic story about how I came to write it in the first place.

In the late summer of 1931, or it may have been in the early autumn, a thirty-five-year old major in the Grenadier Guards, Boy Browning to his brother-officers, second-in-command to the second battalion of his regiment, said to one of his closest friends in the Grenadiers, 'I've read a novel called *The Loving Spirit*, one of the best books I've read for years, and apparently it's all about Fowey in Cornwall. I'm determined to go down there in my boat Ygdrasil,

'The solitary yachtsman hesitates when he comes upon the mouth of the Creek, for there is something of mystery about it even now, something of enchantment.'

Left: *'The Tree of Fate'. Was it really chance that had brought me to the bottom of Bodinnick hill, and now this boat Ygdrasil and the most attractive man at her helm?*

and see the place for myself. Perhaps I'll have the luck to meet the girl who has written it. How about it? Will you come with me?' John Prescott, the brother-officer, agreed, and together they proceeded down the coast and arrived at Fowey. It was sister Angela who first spotted them.

'There's a most attractive man going up and down the harbour in a white motor-boat,' she said, watching through field-glasses from the hatch window at Ferryside. 'Do come and look.'

Mildly interested, I obeyed the summons. 'H'm,' I said, 'he is rather good.'

The cruising up and down continued through the weeks, and some local gossip informed us that the stunning helmsman was called Browning, and he was said to be the youngest major in the British Army! And that was that. I thought no more about him.

It was not until the following year, 1932, in April, having survived a mild operation for appendicitis, and arriving down in my beloved Fowey to recuperate, that I heard 'Major Browning' was in the harbour and afloat again, having laid-up his boat Ygdrasil with the Bodinnick boat-builder, one of my neighbours, George Hunkin.

Mrs Hunkin was my informant. 'The Major would like to meet you,' she told me, 'He's very nice.'

'Oh?'

I was secretly flattered, and to attract attention had my pram up on the slipway and gave her a coat of varnish. A note in the current diary, on April 7th, says, 'That Browning man kept passing in his boat, but he didn't attempt to do anything. Don't blame him. I sat around and read.'

The following day a note was brought to me by Mrs Hunkin, which, though alas I never kept it, read as follows, to the best of my

Below: *A thirty-five-year old major in the Grenadier Guards, Boy Browning to his brother-officers.*

A photograph of me by Compton Collier at precisely this time, 1932.

belief, 'Dear Miss du Maurier, I believe my late father, Freddie Browning, used to know yours, as fellow-members of the Garrick Club. The Hunkins tell me you have had your appendix out and can't do much rowing yet, so I wondered if you would care to come out in my boat? How about tomorrow afternoon?' I sent word back that I should be delighted.

Friday, April 8th. 'A fine bright day with a cold wind. In the afternoon I went out with Browning in his boat. It was the most terrific fun, the seas short and jumpy, and he put his boat hard into it, and we got drenched with spray. She's called Ygdrasil because he's mad on Norse mythology, and it means the Tree of Fate. His friends call him Boy, but he told me to call him Tommy, which is what his family call him. He's the most amazing person to be with, no effort at all, and I feel I've known him for years. I also showed him all over Marie-Louise, and then we came back, sat over a roaring fire which I lit, talked about everything in the world, and it was the most extraordinary evening I've ever spent.'

The Tree of Fate. . .The next two days we spent entirely in each other's company, then he had to return to his battalion, but in a week he was back again, having driven through the night! I was sawing up some logs early in the morning, and I heard him call to the dog. Hatless, brown-leather jerkin, grey flannel trousers thrust into sea-boots. . .green eyes, and a smile that curled at one corner. Yes, no doubt about it, he was good.

'You seem to get a lot of leave,' I told him.

'Not much going on at the moment,' he said, 'and my commanding-officer enjoys doing all the work. Besides, he happens to be one of my closest friends. Come on. Leave those logs, Yggy is waiting for you.'

I had never been given a direct order before, and I loved it!

So a rapid courtship began, and within a few weeks he became as wedded to Fowey – the harbour, the river, the walks, the people – as I was myself. By the end of June, after frequent visits, we decided to become engaged.

The sun shone for us on the day – July 19th – that we were married. At 8.15 am – time to catch the tide – my parents and I proceeded in our boat up Pont Creek to Lanteglos, Tommy and the Hunkins following in Ygdrasil. Afterwards Mrs Hunkin called me Mrs Browning, which sounded so strange. And when we got back to the harbour everyone seemed to know what had happened, and were waving from houses and cottages. We quickly had breakfast, then loaded stores on to Yggy, and set off for the harbour mouth heading down-channel for the Helford river and Frenchman's Creek. We couldn't have chosen anything more beautiful.

When the east wind blows up Helford river the shining waters become troubled and disturbed, and the little waves beat angrily upon the sandy shores. The short seas break above the bar at ebb-tide, and the waders fly inland to the mud flats, their wings skimming the surface, and calling to one another as they go. Only the gulls remain, wheeling and crying above the foam, diving now and again in search of food, their grey feathers glistening with the salt spray.

The long rollers of the Channel, travelling from beyond Lizard point, follow hard upon the steep seas at the river mouth, and mingling with the surge and wash of deep sea water comes the brown tide, swollen with the last rains and brackish from the mud, bearing upon its face dead twigs and straws, and strange forgotten things, leaves too early fallen, young birds, and the buds of flowers.

The open roadstead is deserted, for an east wind makes uneasy anchorage, and but for the few houses scattered here and there above Helford passage, and the group of bungalows about Port Navas, the river would be the same as it was in a century now forgotten, in a time that has left few memories.

Helford river at ebb-tide. 'The tide was ebbing, the water oozing away from the mud flats . . .'
Frenchman's Creek

In those days the hills and the valleys were alone in splendour, there were no buildings to desecrate the rough fields and cliffs, no chimney pots to peer out of the tall woods. There were a few cottages in Helford hamlet, but they made no impression upon the river life itself, which belonged to the birds – curlew and redshank, guillemot and puffin. No yachts rode to the tide then, as they do today, and that stretch of placid water where the river divides to Constantine and Gweek was calm and undisturbed.

The river was little known, save to a few mariners who have found shelter there when the south-west gales drove them in-shore from their course up-channel, and they found the place lonely and austere, a little frightening because of the silence, and when the wind was fair again were glad to weigh anchor and set sail. Helford hamlet was no inducement to a sailor ashore, the few cottage folk dull-witted and uncommunicative, and the fellow who has been away from warmth and women over-long has little desire to wander in the woods or dabble with the waders in the mud at ebb-tide. So the winding river remained unvisited, the woods and the hills untrodden, and all the drowsy beauty of midsummer that gives Helford river a strange enchantment, was never seen and never known.

Today there are many voices to blunder in upon the silence. The pleasure steamers come and go, leaving a churning wake, and yachtsmen visit one another, and even the day-tripper, his dull eye surfeited with undigested beauty, ploughs in and out amongst the shallows, a prawning net in hand. Sometimes, in a little puffing car, he jerks his way along the uneven, muddy track that leads sharply to the right out of Helford village, and takes his tea with his fellow-trippers in the stone kitchen of the old farm building that once

was Navron House. There is something of grandeur about it even now. Part of the original quadrangle still stands, enclosing the farm-yard of today, and the two pillars that once formed the entrance to the house, now over-grown with ivy and encrusted with lichen, serve as props to the modern barn and its corrugated roof.

The farm kitchen, where the tripper takes his tea, was part of Navron dining-hall, and the little half-stair, now terminating in a bricked-up wall, was the stair leading to the gallery. The rest of the house must have crumbled away, or been demolished, for the square farm-building, though handsome enough, bears little likeness to the Navron of the old prints, shaped like the letter E, and of the formal garden and the park there is no trace today.

The tripper eats his split and drinks his tea, smiling upon the landscape, knowing nothing of the woman who stood there once, long ago, in another summer, who caught the gleam of the river amidst the trees, as he does, and who lifted her head to the sky and felt the sun.

He hears the homely farm-yard noises, the clanking of pails, the lowing of cattle, the rough voices of the farmer and his son as they call to each other across the yard, but his ears are deaf to the echoes of that other time, when someone whistled softly from the dark belt of trees, his hands cupped to his

The trees crowd thick and darkly to the water's edge – 'all the drowsy beauty of midsummer that gives Helford river a strange enchantment'.

mouth, and was swiftly answered by the thin, stooping figure crouching beneath the walls of the silent house, while above them the casement opened, and Dona watched and listened, her hands playing a little nameless melody upon the sill, her ringlets falling forward over her face.

The river flows on, the trees rustle in the summer wind, and down on the mud flats the oyster-catchers stand at ebb-tide scanning the shallows for

Below: *'Sometimes, in a little puffing car, the day-tripper jerks his way along the uneven, muddy track that leads sharply to the right out of Helford village, and takes his tea in the stone kitchen of the old farm building that once was Navron House.'*

Right: *'The two pillars that once formed the entrance to the house.'*

food, and the curlews cry, but the men and women of that other time are forgotten, their head-stones encrusted with lichen and moss, their names indecipherable.

Today the cattle stamp and churn the earth over the vanished porch of Navron House, where once a man stood as the clock struck midnight, his face smiling in the dim candle-light, his drawn sword in his hand.

In spring the farmer's children gathered primroses and snowdrops in the banks above the creek, their muddy boots snapping the dead twigs and the fallen leaves of a spent summer, and the creek itself, swollen with the rains of a long winter, looks desolate and grey.

The trees still crowd thick and darkly to the water's edge, and the moss is succulent and green upon the little quay where Dona built her fire and looked across the flames and laughed at her lover, but today no ship lies at anchor in the pool, with rakish masts pointing to the skies, there is no rattle of chain through the hawse hole, no rich tobacco smell upon the air, no echo of voices coming across the water in a lilting foreign tongue.

The solitary yachtsman who leaves his yacht in the open roadstead of Helford, and goes exploring up-river in his dinghy on a night in midsummer, when the night-jars call, hesitates when he comes upon the mouth of the creek, for there is something of mystery about it even now, something of enchantment. Being a stranger, the yachtsman looks back over his shoulder to the safe yacht in the roadstead, and to the broad waters of the river, and he pauses, resting on his paddles, aware suddenly of the deep silence of the creek, of its narrow twisting channel, and he feels – for no reason known to him – that he is an interloper, a trespasser in time. He ventures a little way along the left bank of the creek, the sound of the blades upon the water seeming over-loud and echoing oddly among the trees on the farther bank, and as he creeps forward the creek narrows, the trees crowd yet more thickly

Dona St Columb walked across the lawn of Navron House, towards 'the belt of trees where the stranger and William had talked . . . their footsteps had made a little track.'

Above: *'She followed the track . . . plunging deep down into the woods . . . The trees were thinning, she was coming to the bank . . .'*

'. . . there, suddenly before her for the first time, was the creek, still and soundless, shrouded by the trees, hidden from the eyes of men . . . This creek was a source of enchantment, a new escape, a place to drowse and sleep, a lotus-land.'

'She went on, coming to the corner where the creek turned. There before her, where the creek suddenly widened, forming a pool, lay a ship at anchor . . . Then she knew, then she understood . . . This was the Frenchman's hiding-place – that was his ship. And then, even as she turned to slip away among the trees, a figure stepped out from behind her . . .'

to the water's edge, and he feels a spell upon him, fascinating, strange, a thing of queer excitement not fully understood.

He is alone, and yet – can that be a whisper, in the shallows, close to the bank, and does a figure stand there, the moonlight glinting upon his buckled shoes and that cutlass in his hand, and is that a woman by his side, a cloak around her shoulders, her dark ringlets drawn back behind her ears? He is wrong, of course, those are only the shadows of the trees, and the whispers are no more than the rustle of the leaves and the stir of a sleeping bird, but he is baffled suddenly, and a little scared, he feels he must go no farther, and that the head of the creek beyond the farther bank is barred to him and must remain unvisited. And so he turns to go, heading the dinghy's nose for the roadstead, and as he pulls away the sounds and the whispers become more insistent to his ears, there comes the patter of footsteps, a call, and a cry in the night, a far faint whistle, and a curious lilting song. He strains his eyes in the darkness, and the massed shadows before him loom hard and clear like the outline of a ship. A thing of grace and beauty, born in another time, a painted phantom ship. And now his heart begins to beat, and he strains at his paddles, and the little dinghy shoots swiftly over the dark water away from enchantment, for what he has seen is not of his world, and what he has heard is beyond his understanding.

Once more he reaches the security of his own ship, and looking back for the last time to the entrance of the creek, he sees the full moon white and shining in all its summer glory rise above the tall trees, bathing the creek in loveliness and light.

A night-jar churrs from the bracken on the hills, a fish breaks the surface of the water with a little plopping sound, and slowly his ship turns to meet the incoming tide, and the creek is hidden from him.

The yachtsman goes below to the snug security of his cabin, and browsing amongst his books he finds at last the thing for which he has been searching. It is a map of Cornwall, ill-drawn and inaccurate, picked up in an idle moment in a Truro bookshop. The parchment is faded and yellow, the markings indistinct. The spelling belongs to another century. Helford river is traced fairly enough, and so are the hamlets of Constantine and Gweek. But the yachtsman looks away from them to the marking of a narrow inlet, branching from the parent river, its short, twisting course running westward into a valley. Someone has scratched the name in thin faded characters – Frenchman's Creek.

The yachtsman puzzles awhile over the name, then shrugs his shoulders and rolls away the map. Presently he sleeps. The anchorage is still. No wind blows upon the water, and the night-jars are silent. The yachtsman dreams – and as the tide surges gently about his ship and the moon shines on the quiet river, soft murmurs come to him, and the past becomes the present.

A forgotten century peers out of dust and cobwebs and he walks in another time. He hears the sound of hoof-beats galloping along the drive to Navron House, he sees the great door swing open and the white, startled face of the manservant stare upward at the cloaked horseman. He sees Dona come to the head of the stairs, dressed in her old gown, with a shawl about her head, while down in the silent hidden creek a man walks the deck of his ship, his hands behind his back, and on his lips a curious secret smile. The farm kitchen of Navron House is a dining-hall once more, and someone crouches on the stairs, a knife in his hand, while from above there rings suddenly the startled cry of a child, and down upon the crouching figure a shield crashes from the walls of the gallery, and two little King Charles spaniels, perfumed and curled, run yapping and screaming to the body on the floor.

On Midsummer Eve a wood fire burns on a deserted quay, and a man and a woman look at one another and smile and acknowledge their secret, and at dawn a ship sails with the tide, and the sun shines fiercely from a bright blue sky, and the sea-gulls cry.

All the whispers and echoes from a past that is gone teem into the sleeper's brain, and he is with them, and part of them; part of the sea, the ship, the walls of Navron House, part of a carriage that rumbles and lurches in the rough roads of Cornwall, part even of that lost forgotten London, artificial, painted, where link-boys carried flares, and tipsy gallants laughed at the corner of a cobbled mud-splashed street. He sees Harry in his satin coat, his spaniels at his heels, blundering into Dona's bedroom, as she places the rubies in her ears. He sees William with his button mouth, his small inscrutable face. And last he sees *La Mouette* at anchor in a narrow twisting

stream, he sees the trees at the water's edge, he hears the heron and the curlew cry, and lying on his back asleep he breathes and lives the lovely folly of that lost midsummer which first make the creek a refuge, and a symbol of escape.

FRENCHMAN'S CREEK

Today, if you sail the Helford during the magic moments before dusk falls, you can – even today, nearly half a century since the novel was published – experience something of its mystery and enchantment. As you head down-river, the tide slackens, the trees darken, the birds are hushed, there is no sound except the whisper

'As the solitary yachtsman creeps forward the creek narrows, the trees crowd yet more thickly to the water's edge, and he feels a spell upon him, fascinating, strange, a thing of queer excitement not fully understood.'

of water past the anchor chain until, if the yachtsman is lucky, he may yet hear the night-jar call. It is a summons unlike any other, churring, low, strangely compelling, so that on first hearing it you must think of neither bird nor beast but of some forgotten species, a scaly lizard cross-bred with a toad. There is no sweetness here, no nightingale passion, no owl foreboding; the call is primitive, insistent, with a rhythmic rise and fall, coming not from the wooded slopes but from the open ground beyond, where amidst foxglove and gorse the night-jar crouches.

The title of my novel – *Frenchman's Creek* – was not original: Q had used it many years before in one of his short stories, and graciously gave me permission to use it again, saying, if I remember rightly, that he looked forward to seeing what I had made of it. In hindsight it seems less of a coincidence that he 'touched' all three of the novels which speak of the primaeval spirit of Cornwall – *Jamaica Inn*, *Frenchman's Creek*, and the novel on which we collaborated, *Castle Dor*, based upon the ancient Cornish legend of Tristan and Iseult. These, more than any other of my novels, are about the mythic history, the mystery, the primaeval enchantment that make this land and its people what they are. Q had begun to write *Castle Dor* in the 1920s, a time when other writers invoked legend and mythology in their work – T S Eliot in *The Waste Land*, James Joyce in *Ulysses*. But whereas these writers used myths and legends – including that of Tristan – as a creative device to stimulate the imagination and to try to make sense of the modern

The 'ancient cirque' of Castle Dor – 5th-century fortress-palace of King Mark of ancient myth. 'Let me tell you something. Some nineteen years ago I was waiting up at Castle Dor for a child to make its appearance in the world and as I vigiled under the stars it seemed to me that I was near to stumbling upon something . . . It had no dimensions, small or great . . . what it was I could not say, the secret was beyond me.'

In search of King Mark's house I found, on an old map, a field named Mark's Gate, which led to Lantyan Farm. 'Cannot you see? A field in the very place entered as "Mark's Gate" – "Mark's Gate"! Oh! It's a clincher! And Woodgate would be t'other approach from the river . . .'
Castle Dor

world, Q maintained no such ironic distance. He was a Cornishman through and through; for the Cornishman his legends are part of the reality of being Cornish, they are his inheritance. While I felt his novel worth preserving for its description of the Fowey countryside alone, it was his belief – that a soil once having brought to birth such a story of Tristan and Iseult would 'be unable to forget or desist from the effort to throw up secondary shoots' – that convinced me.

It was fourteen years after the death of Sir Arthur that his daughter Foy asked me to resolve and finish the manuscript of *Castle Dor*. Clearly Q had intended a romance in his own Troy town between Linnet, the wife of an Inkeeper, and Amyot, a Breton onion-seller; and that, further, these two were meant to re-enact, in a more modern setting, the parts of Tristan and Iseult of ancient myth. According to the Tristan legend, Mark, or Marcus, was a king of Cornwall during the sixth century or possibly earlier. The legend is one of seduction and betrayal, King Mark, Iseult and Tristan forming a triangle of jealous husband, faithless wife and ardent lover respectively, the two young people bent on deceit.

Q had it from Professor Loth, who had transcribed it from the earliest extant manuscript of the Tristan series – *Le Roman de Tristan* by the twelfth-century chronicler Beroul – that King Mark's palace was at Lancien (ancient rendering of Lantyan) now

Woodget Pyll. The old people in the neighbourhood called the stream Deraine Lake (Lac de la Reine?). A king, they said, (King Mark?) had made it for his queen (Iseult?) and put swans upon it, where still they breed today.

'The old people said that if anyone dipped a fork into it and stuck his fork into the red sand, a thunderstorm would come up, and a wind so roaring that it stripped all the leaves off the trees.'

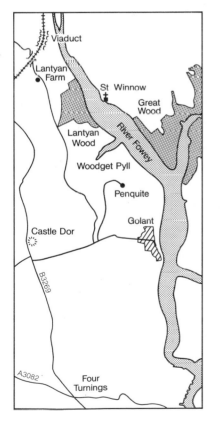

a farmstead close to the Fowey River by Castle Dor. Excavation in 1936 and 1937 on the site of Castle Dor proved the scholars right. Here, beyond all doubt, was the original Lancien, fortress-palace of King Mark, husband of Iseult. It is also possible that on the site where the farmhouse now stands, or nearer to the river, the King had a separate dwelling-place, with the Queen's quarters beside it, giving more shelter and greater privacy than did the soldier's garrison at Castle Dor.

One of my first reactions to the proposal that I should complete Q's manuscript was to send for every available volume on the legend of Tristan and Iseult from the London Library. Here was my downfall for there are divers versions and I was soon bemused by them all. The essential story, which readers of the novel may find useful in appreciating the modern parallel of Amyot and Linnet, suggests that Tristan was King Mark's nephew and served him as a knight.

The story goes that Morholt, brother of the Queen of Ireland, arrived in Cornwall, boldly demanding tribute to the Irish King in the form of slaves. Tristan challenges him to combat on the Island of St Sampson. Morholt is mortally wounded by a splinter of Tristan's sword which lodges in his skull.

(How often Tommy and I – the search for Tristan constantly in mind – strolled beside Woodget Pyll and up to the lane above, beside Lantyan Woods, past Lantyan Farm and down to the

Left: *Lantyan Farm, below Castle Dor, could well have been built on the site of King Mark's private dwelling place. 'I believe, as Beroul knew, that Iseult and Tristan loved and suffered on the very spot . . . Be prepared though for a mere farmhouse – no palace!'*

Linnet (Iseult) and Deborah (Brangwyn) row up river to meet Amyot (Tristan), 'their excuse being that they were to attend evening service at St Winnow. They passed the church a good hour before its bell would ring for service, . . . and flooded up almost to the arches of a railway viaduct beneath Lantyan.'

'Here, at the base of the wooded hill, where the great railway viaduct stood today, Iseult had waited in the moonlight, while the shadow of her lover, Tristan, his finger to his lips warned her to be silent, for the king her husband was hiding near at hand.'

further creek beneath the viaduct, and wondered whether one of the islands formed by the mud-flats in the creek when the tide withdraws, could have been the fighting ground of Tristan and Morholt.)

Following the combat, in which Tristan is also injured, he finds that his wound will not heal. Trusting in fate, he casts himself to the winds in a boat and lands in Ireland. Realising where he is, and the danger to himself in being recognised, he adopts the disguise of a minstrel by the name of Tantris (an anagram of Tristan). His wound is healed by Iseult, the King of Ireland's daughter, and Tristan returns to Cornwall.

Convinced by his advisors that he should produce an heir before he dies, King Mark decides to marry, and chooses as his wife the woman – whoever she may be – whose hair a swallow has let fall from its beak. The search for the woman leads Tristan back to Ireland where he slays a dragon that is terrorising the kingdom. As a reward the King of Ireland pardons him for killing Morholt and offers Tristan his daughter, Iseult, in marriage, but when Tristan discovers that Iseult is also the object of his search for a wife for King Mark, he determines to take her back to fulfil her destiny.

Before they set off for Cornwall, the Queen of Ireland brews a love potion which she gives to Brangwyn, Iseult's maid, for use on Iseult's wedding night. But on the voyage to Cornwall, Brangwyn gives the potion (some say mistakenly) to Tristan and Iseult to drink. They fall in love, consummate the affair and persuade Brangwyn to take Iseult's place on her wedding night.

The island in the creek beneath the viaduct – fighting ground of Tristan and Morholt? 'It was an island . . . cut off from the shore by a narrow channel across which one could toss a stone: a long, narrow eyot of two furlongs or less with undercut banks of mud.'

After Mark and Iseult are married, Tristan and Iseult carry on their affair, the King's response alternating between belief in their protested innocence and anger at their more apparent deception. On one occasion Mark has flour spread before Iseult's bed, but Tristan avoids leaving a tell-tale imprint of his foot in the flour by leaping into the connubial couch from sprinting distance. On another – interesting to readers of *Castle Dor* (and, indeed, *Rebecca*) – Mark discovers the couple asleep in the forest of Moroi – the Happy Valley, a sort of paradise for lovers – but interprets their lying apart from one another as a sign of verisimilitude. Mark leaves his glove, a ring and a sword to show that he has been there.

After three years the power of the potion abates, but pursued by the King's men once more, Tristan flees to Brittany where, to console himself and despite real love for Iseult, he marries the daughter of the ruler of the kingdom (the Duke of Hoel), rather confusingly also called Iseult – Iseult of the White Hands.

When King Mark makes further proclamation for Tristan's life, Tristan responds by returning to Cornwall to tell his full story, in the disguise of a madman named Picous. But the dog, Husdant, that Tristan had given to Iseult, recognises him. Tristan re-unites fleetingly with Iseult before escaping, mortally injured, back to Brittany.

Once in France, he sends for Iseult, believing that she alone can cure him. If Tristan's messenger succeeds in persuading Iseult to come to his aid he is to return with white sails on his ship; if not they are to be black. Iseult sets out for Brittany immediately, but as the ship comes into sight, Iseult of the White Hands tricks

The long stone which once marked the site of Tristan's tomb. It can be seen on the road to Fowey, just below Four Turnings.

The action moves to the home of Tristan's friend, Dinas of Lidon, Castle-an-Dinas.
'The brougham emerged on to the great high road from Bodmin to Truro . . . "Bear right soon after we pass the turning to Roche,"
called Mr Tregentil . . . "Our road should be marked St Columb."'

Tristan into believing that the sails are black. Tristan dies, heartbroken, and Iseult collapses too as she holds his dead body in her arms.

There are so many versions of the legend that purists will find fault with any one. Beroul's version, on which Amyot and Linnet's story is largely based, was left unfinished by its author. The ending attributed to him, but in fact the imaginative work of later writers, can therefore certainly be discounted. Another interpretation has the maid Brangwyn betray her mistress to King Mark, who, coming upon Tristan singing to the queen, wounds him with a poisoned spear, and locks Iseult in her chamber to prevent her following her lover. Tristan flies to his friend Dinas of Lidon, and dies at his castle – Castle an Dinas, the finest hill castle in all Cornwall. And in the novel, it is here that Doctor Carfax makes his fatal attempt to free Amyot (Tristan) from 'that double-headed monster of damnation and salvation – Time'.

Dinas, friend to Iseult and Tristan, seneschal to his overlord King Mark, paced up and down this piece of territory once, his dwelling-house perhaps where the sheds stood now, or even beneath the engine-house itself, topped by the chimney yonder. Miners drained the lode, deep in the earth, beside which, centuries since, the servants toiled, and the disused shaft amidst the furze a few yards or so ahead ringed about with rotten fencing, might have seemed – to a traveller in time who knew his way – the entrance to a stairway.

The hoof prints ceased, the muddied ground was trampled, as if the horse had taken fright and fled, and straight to the shaft through the furze lay the new-beaten track. Nor was the fencing rotted. The posts leant sideways because they had been smashed.

'Amyot!' called Doctor Carfax, 'Amyot!'

The echo mocked him, flung back from the empty sheds, and in the mist and darkness the chimney stack loomed larger than before. It seemed to the doctor, standing there by the black pit which perhaps less than a dozen years or so ago had served as a mine shaft and been discontinued, that he hovered now in strange and sickening fashion on the threshold of another world. Whatever he said or did in the present time would only be repetition of a day gone by, and anyone who listened to his voice calling in the darkness would hear it as the voice of another, dead these thirteen hundred years.

'Trestane!' he called. 'Trestane!' and the sound of the changed name was not foolish in his ears, but strangely ominous, for the echo came back to him without the sharpness of his first cry. Now with a melancholy haunting note, the widely flung 'Trestane' sounded and died, and the echo was a whisper scarcely louder than a sigh.

Then, gripping his stick firmly in his hands, yet holding his breath with wonder, Doctor Carfax watched a figure rise slowly from the pit beyond him, climbing hand over hand from the depths, now slipping, now secure, and there was black mud about his head and shoulders, and blood upon his face, and the eyes were wild and staring, the eyes of Amyot.

'Who calls?'

The voice, half strangled in a sob, was faint and breathless, and the doctor, knowing that a sudden move and one false step would send the climber back to the unknown depths from which he struggled, remained motionless, knee-deep in the furze beside the broken barricade.

'It is I, Dinas,' he said softly, 'Dinas, your friend.'

The boy stared back at him without recognition, and clinging with one hand to the more solid earth above him, thrust back with his free hand the matted hair that fell about his eyes.

'You've played me false,' said Amyot, 'you or some other. The stairway's gone. They've dug a pit to trap me and I'm held.'

The doctor, leaning forward, saw that the lad's left foot was enmeshed in wire, and if he bent to clear it he would fall.

'Steady,' he said. 'Hold fast with both your hands. I'll come and free you,' and was moving towards the brink, when Amyot shouted: 'Keep back, for I'll not trust you. The fox is abroad tonight and all his men. Dinas serves his king before he serves his friend.'

Suddenly, with a supreme effort, he kicked his foot clear from the tangling wire, and, grasping the edge of the pit, dragged himself to safety.

'Good lad,' cried the doctor. 'Here, seize my stick,' but his leap forward into time proved his undoing, for Amyot, taking both words and gesture as hostile to himself, and the stick as a weapon, sprang sideways, and in a second had flung his whole weight upon his unsuspecting ally. Together they wrestled in the furze, each fighting for supremacy, not three yards from the open shaft, and Carfax, no longer held by the past, knew that, unless he overcame his assailant, death would take him in the present.

Already Amyot, in his blind rage and fear of what he thought betrayal, had

Right: The tin mine at the foot of the castle, possibly the site of Dinas' house – 'perhaps where the sheds stood now, or even beneath the engine-house itself, topped by the chimney yonder.'

Right: '"Look, I think that's it, away yonder, like a hump on the skyline, that's Castle-an-Dinas..."
'Dinas, friend to Iseult and Tristan, seneschal to his overlord King Mark, paced up and down this piece of territory once.'

Tresaddern Farm, 'the comforting grey farm-house' below the castle, where Amyot and party intend to stay.

seized the clasp-knife from the doctor's pocket; already it lay open in his hand and pointing at the doctor's throat, when the older man, forcing back the wrist that threatened him, threw his opponent on his side, so driving the knife into his shoulder by mischance. The blood spurted, and as Amyot cried out in pain the cry released his anger and his fear. He ceased struggling, and was still. Then, drawing the knife from the swift-bleeding wound, he stared back at his late enemy in wonder.

'Doctor Carfax,' he said, 'what have you done to me?'

The doctor did not answer, but flinging off overcoat and jacket proceeded to divest himself of his own cambric shirt, and tear it into strips to staunch the wound.

'There, lad,' he said. 'Keep still, I'll bind you, somewhat rough and ready, but it must suffice' – his voice calm and steady that scarce three minutes since had been nigh choked out of him as he struggled for existence; but even as he spoke, with practised hands applied the only possible dressing of clean

Left: *'It seemed to the doctor that he hovered on the threshold of another world.'*

The hill castles of the first centuries AD were defensive earthworks sometimes three trenches deep. 'Those great banks were treacherous, making the circle seem a prison; Mary could think of no worse fate than to twist an ankle and lie alone here, staring at the sky.'

handkerchief, with strapping of cambric shirt, the dark stain spread down the forearm, and Amyot fainted.

As Doctor Carfax knelt there in the furze at Royalton, beside the disused mine-shaft, and halloed with all the strength in his lungs for Dingle the coachman, or Tregantil his patient, to come to his aid and so help bear young Amyot to the barouche (for there would be two to carry to hospital in Bodmin instead of one), he gave no thought to the death he had himself so narrowly escaped. He stared down at the lad who now lay white and senseless in his arms, bleeding from the wound inadvertently given; and it was not the depth of the wound that bothered him, nor the loss of blood that must inevitably follow before the proper dressings could be applied, but the fact that it was his own clasp-knife, used barely an hour ago to take stones from a horse's hoof, and grimy still with mud and grit, that had pierced the tender flesh of Amyot Trestane, thus playing, fatefully and ironically, the role of a long-vanished poisoned spear.

There is in fact good reason to believe that Tristan died in Cornwall rather than in Brittany, for two miles from King Mark's fortress at Castle Dor (on the Fowey road below Four Turnings),

there stands a pillar, some seven feet high, which carries the inscription 'Drustans Hic Iacit/Cvnomori Filius'. Commorus, or Quonomorius, has been identified by scholars as Marcus, or Mark, King of Cornwall, and Drustans as Tristan, so for those of us less lettered who look upon it the inscription translates, 'Tristan Lies Here, Son of Mark', suggesting further that if the love story is true it is even closer and more elicit than the chroniclers told.

Besides the difficulties thrown up by the conflicting legends, there was the additional problem in resolving Castle Dor that its

My husband, with a soldier's professional eye and an appreciation of high ground, declared that Castle-an-Dinas and Castle Dor could have been held in old days against all comers. '"It commanded the whole of Cornwall, and was obviously quite impregnable," said Mr Tregantil.'

characters, like step-children, were not my own, their personalities were already formed. One character alone had my full sympathy, and this was Dr Carfax who, like Prospero, appeared to control events, and reminded me so much of Q himself. Surely something of Q's own excitement at discovering King Mark's palace at Lantyan is contained in Dr Carfax's realisation that 'all my boyhood – bird's nesting, blackberrying, nutting, or merely loafing and dreaming – I had been treading the very tracks of one of the greatest love stories in the world.' The great Cornishman's close relationship with the country of his forefathers and his strong sense that myths and legends get at something universal -'old, unhappy, far-off things' – about this ancient land, seemed to place him in Carfax's position in the novel. For it is Carfax (a name derived from an old French word 'carrefures' meaning the place where all roads lead), who in some strange way sets in motion the whole story – the re-enactment of the Tristan legend by Amyot and Linnet. In the prologue to the novel, Carfax stands under the stars at Castle Dor, waiting for the baby Linnet to be born. Imbued with the primaeval spirit of the site he breathes into Linnet his sense of its haunting tragedy, thereby dooming her to unwilling repetition of a life that is not hers.

Many years ago, in the early 1840s, on an October night very clear and lustrous, a certain Doctor Carfax stood sentry with a field-telescope upon the earthwork of Castle Dor in Cornwall. He had arrived on a summons to the blacksmith's at the crossroads near by, the blacksmith's wife being in labour.

The inner circle covers some acre and a half of land with space for stabling, granaries, bakehouses, dining-chambers, sleeping-quarters and a whole army of warriors.

He had arrived to find the travail going well and naturally: and being a one who believed in nature being left to herself, put his bag on the kitchen chair, and strolled off across a dewy meadow, having told the competent midwife to hail him when necessary. After a while on the earthwork, which lay but a field away from the forge, the doctor, accustomed to such vigils, found himself passing familiarly enough through three stages of sensation, to arrive upon a fourth at once novel and most magical.

First came the feeling of aloofness which, while it seems to be regal enough, belongs to any man of ordinary imagination who stands on a high ridge under stars. They are a crown we can all fit upon us, to cheat us into derisory thoughts of this planet and a mood in which all man's fret upon it becomes as a weaving of midges beneath a summer bough. This mood contains its own rebuke. Being men, we belong to earth: belonging to earth, like Archimedes, we must stand somewhere: and wherever we stand to play at astronomers, it is a condition that we cannot be aware of what hovers at our feet.

Ignoring these considerations, and still intent on the firmament – where over the plain of the sea Sirius sparkled as a flint under the heel of the Hunter, Aldebaran was a ruby and the Pleiads aloft on its right hung like a cobweb in the cross-moon-shine – Doctor Carfax passed to a second apprehension again familiar – of the vast dome inexorably, almost visibly turning, and of our earth (himself with it) spinning 'widdershins' or back-somersaulting beneath it, at incredible speed.

This (for he was a commonsensical man, albeit imaginative) hitched him back to his feet – to be aware of the dark brambles around him covering grass-blades innumerable and minute leaflets of the thyme by the million; these in turn covering asleep the insect life to be released in its myriads next summer and fill the air and all the field with humming. Of a sudden our world grew enormous again – a rounded world with curved uplands that dipped to the sea's more gradual curve. The sea itself . . . .

the great sea
Lay, a strong vessel at his master's gate,
And, like a drunken giant, sobbed in sleep.

No – Sea and Land were giant and giantess, rather, locked in exhaustion after tremendous embraces: and it seemed to him – now turned from watcher to listener – that while the giant audibly snored, his mate could not sleep: that her bosom heaved with an inarticulate trouble, a word that could not be told; and somehow that the secret was meant for *him*, and concerned men and women just here where he stood. Yet it could not concern – it was too important to concern – any of the folk who slept in the valley cottages beneath him or the immediate trouble at the forge-house nearby on the high road, or anyone in the vale below him there who perchance lay awake remembering a sorrow locked away in this or that folded churchyard among the hills . . . He knew – as who but a medical practitioner can know – these folk.

I believed this novel worth preserving for Q's belief that 'a soil once having brought to birth such a story of Tristan and Iseult would never so flower again, yet be unable to forget or desist from the effort to throw up secondary shoots.'

Nurtured on this soil, his young eyes having fed on this very landscape, he had in fact caused a repetition of one of the saddest love stories in the world.

No, again. This most ancient cirque of Castle Dor, deserted, bramble-grown, was the very nipple of a huge breast in pain, aching for discharge.

Day broke slowly – closing a shutter on space to open another on time. For the rampart overlooks on the one hand a bay of the sea, on the other a river ford deep-set in a vale. From a nook of the bay, centuries ago, a *soi-disant* Caesar pushed out with his ships to win Rome. In a field sloping northward from the ramp, the guns and foot of a Parliament Army capitulated to King Charles on his last campaign of the West. The king had his coach anchored under the lee of a hedge yonder, and slept in it on the night before the surrender. Across the ford below regiments have stormed and shouted.

But these memories lifted themselves with the valley mists, to dissolve and trail away over woodland, arable, pasture; and he knew that it was not for any secret of theirs he had been listening, nor yet for any lowly tale decipherable of quarrel, ancient feud, litigation, which had parcelled the fields at his feet or twisted the parish roads. All England is a palimpsest of such, scored over with writ of hate and love, begettings of children beneath the hazels, betrayals, appeals, curses, concealed travails. But this was different somehow. It had no dimensions, small or great. In a way it had escaped dimensions, to be universal; and yet just here – here, waiting . . . An owl hooted up from the woods. A titlark on a stone announced the day. A moment later in the daylight the blacksmith, coming across the meadow, panted that all was well but he was wanted. Doctor Carfax closed his telescope, musing, and retraced his steps to the forge. The word, for a moment so close upon utterance, had escaped him.

CHAPTER FOUR

THE CALAMITY OF YESTERDAY

~

But to what purpose
Disturbing the dust on a bowl of rose-leaves
I do not know

Other echoes
Inhabit the garden. Shall we follow?
Quick, said the bird, find them, find them,
Round the corner. . .

T S ELIOT

When I first stayed at Ferryside I would seize every opportunity to explore, to walk for miles – bluebells everywhere – or cross the ferry to Fowey, walk through the town, and so to the castle on the cliff above the harbour mouth. Soon I discovered with fascination the enchanted woods on the Gribben headland, and one day looking north, inland from the Gribben, I could just make out the grey roof of a house set in its own grounds in the midst of the trees.

That would be Menabilly, I was told. Belongs to Dr Rashleigh, but he seldom lives there. Apparently the property had been first built in the reign of Queen Elizabeth, the grounds and woods had been in the last century famous for their beauty, and the property had never changed hands from the time it came into being, but had passed down, in the male line, to the present owner.

It was an afternoon in late autumn, the first time I tried to find the house. October, November, the month escapes me. But in the west country autumn can make herself a witch, and place a spell upon the walker. The trees were golden brown, the hydrangeas had massive heads still blue and untouched by flecks of wistful grey, and I would set forth at three of an afternoon with foolish notions of August still in my head. 'I will strike inland,' I thought, 'and come back by way of the cliffs, and the sun will yet be high, or at worst touching the horizon beyond the western hills.'

We set forth, Angela and I, with a panting Pekinese held by a leash. We came to the lodge at Four Turnings, as we had been told, and opened the creaking iron gates with the flash courage and

I would seize every opportunity to explore, to walk for miles – bluebells everywhere. Soon I discovered with fascination the enchanted woods on the Gribben headland.

appearance of bluff common to the trespasser. The lodge was deserted. No one peered at us from the windows. We slunk away down the drive, and were soon hidden by the trees. I remember we did not talk, or if we did we talked in whispers. That was the first effect the woods had upon both of us.

The drive twisted and turned in a way that I described many years afterwards, when sitting at a desk in Alexandria and looking out upon a hard glazed sky and dusty palm trees; but on that first autumnal afternoon, when the drive was new to us, it had the magic quality of a place hitherto untrodden, unexplored. I was Scott in the Antarctic. I was Cortez in Mexico. Or possibly I was none of these things, but a trespasser in time. The woods were sleeping now, but who, I wondered, had ridden through them once? What hoofbeats had sounded and then died away? What carriage wheels had rolled and vanished? Doublet and hose. Boot and jerkin. Patch and powder. Stock and patent leather. Crinoline and bonnet.

The trees grew taller and the shrubs more menacing. Yet still the drive led on, and never a house at the end of it. Suddenly Angela

It had the magic quality of a place hitherto untrodden, unexplored. I was a trespasser in time.

The woods were sleeping now, but who, I wondered, had ridden through them once? What carriage wheels had rolled and vanished?

said, 'It's after four . . . and the sun's gone.' The Pekinese watched her, pink tongue lolling. And then he stared into the bushes, pricking his ears at nothing. The first owl hooted. . . .

'I don't like it,' said Angela firmly. 'Let's go home.'

'But the house,' I said with longing, 'we haven't seen the house.'

She hesitated, and I dragged her on. But in an instant the day was gone from us. The drive was a muddied path, leading nowhere, and the shrubs, green no longer but a shrouding black, turned to fantastic shapes and sizes. There was not one owl now, but twenty. And through the dark trees, with a pale grin upon his face, came the first glimmer of the livid hunter's moon.

I knew then that I was beaten. For that night only.

'All right,' I said grudgingly, 'we'll find the house another time.'

And, following the moon's light, we struck through the trees and came out upon the hillside. In the distance below us stretched the sea. Behind us the woods and the valley through which we had come. But nowhere was there a sign of any house. Nowhere at all.

'Perhaps,' I thought to myself, 'it is a house of secrets, and has no wish to be disturbed.' But I knew I should not rest until I had found it.

If I remember rightly the weather broke after that day, and the autumn rains were upon us. Driving rain, day after day. And we, not yet become acclimatised to Cornish wind and weather, packed

I would be out in a boat most days, with a line in the water, and it did not matter much what came on the end of it.

up and returned to London for the winter. But I did not forget the woods of Menabilly, or the house that waited. . . .

We came back again Cornwall in the following spring, and I was seized with a fever for fishing. I would be out in a boat most days, with a line in the water, and it did not matter much what came on the end of it, whether it would be seaweed or a dead crab, as long as I could sit on the thwart of a boat and hold a line and watch the sea. The boatman sculled off the little bay called Pridmouth, and as I looked at the land beyond, and saw the massive trees climbing from the valley to the hill, the shape of it all seemed familiar.

'What's up there, in the trees?' I said.

'That's Menabilly,' came the answer, 'but you can't see the house from the shore. It's away up yonder. I've never been there myself.' I felt a bite on my line at that moment and said no more. But the lure of Menabilly was upon me once again.

Next morning I did a thing I had never done before, nor ever did again, except once in the desert, where to see sunrise is the peak of all experience. In short, I rose at 5.00 am. I pulled across the harbour in my pram, walked through the sleeping town, and climbed out upon the cliffs just as the sun himself climbed out on Pont Hill behind me. The sea was glass. The air was soft and misty warm. And the only other creature out of bed was a fisherman, hauling crab pots at the harbour mouth. It gave me a fine feeling of

The only other creature out of bed was a fisherman, hauling crab pots at the harbour mouth.

The solitary cottage by Pridmouth Cove, which became Rebecca's 'half cottage, half boat-house, built of the same stone as the breakwater'.

conceit, to be up before the world. My feet in sand shoes seemed like wings. I came down to Pridmouth Bay, passing the solitary cottage by the lake, and, opening a small gate hard by, I saw a narrow path leading to the woods. Now, at last, I had the day before me, and no owls, no moon, no shadows could turn me back.

I followed the path to the summit of the hill and then, emerging from the woods, turned left, and found myself upon a high grass walk, with all the bay stretched out below me and the Gribben head beyond.

I paused, stung by the beauty of that first pink glow of sunrise on the water, but the path led on, and I would not be deterred. Then I saw them for the first time – the scarlet rhododendrons. Massive and high they reared above my head, shielding the entrance to a long smooth lawn. I was hard upon it now, the place I sought. Some instinct made me crouch upon my belly and crawl softly to

I found myself upon a high grass walk, with all the bay stretched out before below me and the Gribben head beyond.

the wet grass at the foot of the shrubs. The morning mist was lifting, and the sun was coming up above the trees even as the moon had done last autumn. This time there was no owl, but blackbird, thrush and robin greeting the summer day.

I edged my way on to the lawn, and there she stood. My house of secrets. My elusive Menabilly. . .

The windows were shuttered fast, white and barred. Ivy covered the grey walls and threw tendrils round the windows. The house, like the world, was sleeping too. But later, when the sun was high, there would come no wreath of smoke from the chimneys. The shutters would not be thrown back, or the doors unfastened. No voices would sound within those darkened rooms. Menabilly would sleep on, like the sleeping beauty of the fairy tale, until someone should come to wake her.

I watched her awhile in silence, and then became emboldened,

Then I saw for the first time – the scarlet rhododendrons. Massive and high they reached above my head.

and walked across the lawn and stood beneath the windows. The scarlet rhododendrons encircled her lawns, to south, to east, to west. Behind her, to the north, were the tall trees and the deep woods. She was a two-storied house, and with the ivy off her would have a classical austerity that her present shaggy covering denied her.

One of her nineteenth-century owners had taken away her small-paned windows and given her plate glass instead, and he had also built at her northern end an ugly wing that conformed ill with the rest of her. But with all her faults, most obvious to the eye, she had a grace and charm that made me hers upon the instant. She was, or so it seemed to me, bathed in a strange mystery. She held a secret – not one, not two, but many – that she withheld from many people but would give to one who loved her well.

As I sat on the edge of the lawn and stared at her I felt as many romantic, foolish people have felt about the Sphinx. Here was a block of stone, even as the desert Sphinx, made by man for his own purpose – yet she had a personality that was hers alone, without the touch of human hand. One family only had lived within her walls. One family who had given her life. They had been born there, they had loved, they had quarrelled, they had suffered, they had died. And out of these emotions she had woven a personality for herself, she had become what their thoughts and their desires had made her.

And now the story was ended. She lay there in her last sleep. Nothing remained for her but to decay and die. . . .

Who can affirm or deny that the houses which have sheltered us as children, or as adults, and our predecessors too, do not have embedded in their walls, one with the dust and cobwebs, one with the overlay of fresh wallpaper and paint, the imprint of what-has-been, the suffering, the joy?

There was one room that held my fancy most. Dark panels. A great fireplace.

I cannot recollect, now, how long I lay and stared at her. It was past noon, perhaps, when I came back to the living world. I was empty and lightheaded, with no breakfast inside me. But the house possessed me from that day, even as a mistress holds her lover.

Ours was a strange relationship for fifteen years. I would put her from my mind for months at a time, and then, on coming again to Cornwall, I would wait a day or two, then visit her in secret.

Once again I would sit on the lawn and stare up at her windows. Sometimes I would find that the caretaker at the lodge, who came now and again to air the house, had left a blind pulled back, showing a chink of space, so that by pressing my face to the window I could catch a glimpse of a room. There was one room – a dining room, I judged, because of the long sideboard against the wall – that held my fancy most. Dark panels. A great fireplace. And on the walls the family portraits stared into the silence and the dust. Another room, once a library, judging by the books upon the shelves, had become a lumber place, and in the centre of it stood a great dappled rocking horse with scarlet nostrils. What little blue-sashed, romping children once bestrode his back? Where was the laughter gone? Where were the voices that had called along the passages?

Little by little I gleaned snatches of family history. There was the lady in blue who looked, so it was said, from a side window, yet few had seen her face. There was the Cavalier found beneath the buttress wall more than a hundred years ago. There were the sixteenth-century builders, merchants and traders: there were the Stuart royalists, who suffered for their king; the Tory landowners with their white wigs and their brood of children; the Victorian garden lovers with their rare plants and their shrubs.

I saw them all, in my mind's eye, down to the present owner, who could not love his home; and when I thought of him it was not of an elderly man, a respectable justice of the peace, but of a small boy orphaned at two years old, coming for his holidays in an Eton collar and tight black suit, watching his old grandfather with nervous, doubtful eyes. The house of secrets. The house of stories.

One autumn evening I found a window unclasped in the ugly north wing at the back. It must have been intuition that made me bring my torch with me that day. I threw open the creaking window and climbed in. Dust. Dust everywhere. The silence of death. I flashed my torch on to the cobwebbed walls and walked the house. At last. I had imagined it so often. Here were the rooms, leading from one to another, that I had pictured only from outside. Here was the staircase, and the faded crimson wall. There the long drawing room, with its shiny chintz sofas and chairs, and here the dining room, a forgotten corkscrew still lying on the sideboard.

Suddenly the shadows became too many for me, and I turned and went back the way I had come. Softly I closed the window behind me. And as I did so, from a broken pane on the floor above my head came a great white owl, who flapped his way into the woods and vanished. . .

Why did a past that I have never known possess me so completely? The people who had lived and died here once at Menabilly . . . even a tumbledown cottage in a deserted plum orchard which Angela and I had come upon during another of our early expeditions to Menabilly. All that remained were the walls, two windows and a hearth. Once, perhaps two hundred years ago, a woman had bent over that same hearth and stood at the windows, watching. Mournful, mournful. Always the past, just out of reach, waiting to be recaptured. Why did I feel so sad thinking of a past I had never known?

It is now fifty years since my novel, *Rebecca*, was first published. It became the favourite of practically every reader of my books, which surprises me because when I was writing it I didn't think that it was going to sell especially well.

I was thirty years old when I began the story. In the fall of 1937 my soldier husband was commanding officer of the Second Battalion, Grenadier Guards, which was stationed in Alexandria,

The tumbledown cottage that Angela and I discovered during an early expedition to Menabilly. There is no fever like the quest for the past, as warming to the blood as a dig for hidden treasure. If I hadn't been a writer, perhaps I'd have been an archaeologist – digging, always digging!

and I was with him. We were living in a rented home, not far from the beach, Ramleh I believe it was called, and while he was occupied with military matters I was homesick for Cornwall. I think I put a brave face on the situation and went to the various cocktail parties which we were obliged to attend, but all I really wanted to do was write a novel set in my beloved Cornwall.

This novel would not be a tale of smugglers and wreckers of the nineteenth century, like *Jamaica Inn*, but would be set in the present day, say the mid-twenties, and it would be about a young wife and her slightly older husband, living in a beautiful house that had been in his family for generations. There were many such houses in Cornwall; my friend Foy Quiller-Couch, with whom I first visited Jamaica Inn, had taken me to some of them. Houses with extensive grounds, with woods, near to the sea, with family portraits on the walls, like the house Milton in Northamptonshire, where I had stayed as a child during the First World War, and yet not like, because my Cornish house would be empty, neglected, its owner absent, more like – yes, very like Menabilly near Fowey, not so large as Milton, where I had so often trespassed. And surely the Quiller-Couches had once told me that the owner had been married first to a very beautiful wife, whom he had divorced, and had married again a much younger woman?

I wondered if she had been jealous of the first wife, as I would have been jealous if my Tommy had been married before he married me. He had been engaged once, that I knew, and the engagement had been broken off – perhaps she would have been better at dinners and cocktail parties than I could ever be.

Seeds began to drop. A beautiful home . . . a first wife . . . jealousy . . . a wreck, perhaps at sea, near to the house, as there had been at Pridmouth near Menabilly. But something terrible would have to happen, I did not know what. . . . I paced up and down the living room in Alexandria, notebook in hand, nibbling first my nails and then my pencil.

The couple would be living abroad, after some tragedy, there would be an epilogue – but on second thoughts that would have to come at the beginning – the Chapters One, and Two, and Three . . . If only we did not have to go out to dinner that night, I wanted to think. . . .

And my thoughts turned to my first encounter with Menabilly, as I made my way down the old driveway from the east lodge, as it were in a dream.

Last night I dreamt I went to Manderley again. It seemed to me I stood by the iron gate leading to the drive, and for a while I could not enter, for the

Looking across the beach from which Rebecca embarked upon her final voyage.

'It seemed to me I stood by the iron gates leading to the drive, and for a while I could not enter, for the way was barred to me.'

way was barred to me. There was a padlock and a chain upon the gate. I called in my dream to the lodge-keeper, and had no answer, and peering closer through the rusted spokes of the gate I saw that the lodge was uninhabited.

No smoke came from the chimney, and the little lattice windows gaped forlorn. Then, like all dreamers, I was possessed of a sudden with supernatural powers and passed like a spirit through the barrier before me. The drive wound away in front of me, twisting and turning as it had always done, but as I advanced I was aware that a change had come upon it; it was narrow and unkept, not the drive that we had known. At first I was puzzled and did not understand, and it was only when I bent my head to avoid the low swinging branch of a tree that I realised what had happened. Nature had come into her own again and, little by little, in her stealthy, insidious way had encroached upon the drive with long, tenacious fingers. The woods, always a menace even in the past, had triumphed in the end. They crowded, dark and uncontrolled, to the borders of the drive. The beeches with white, naked limbs leant close to one another, their branches intermingled in a strange embrace, making a vault above my head like the archway of a church. And there were other trees as well, trees that I did not recognise, squat oaks and tortured elms that straggled cheek by jowl with the beeches, and had thrust themselves out of the quiet earth, along with monster shrubs and plants, none of which I remembered.

The drive was a ribbon now, a thread of its former self, with gravel surface gone, and choked with grass and moss. The trees had thrown out low branches, making an impediment to progress; the gnarled roots looked like skeleton claws. Scattered here and again amongst this jungle growth I would recognise shrubs that had been landmarks in our time, things of culture and grace, hydrangeas whose blue heads had been famous. No hand had checked their progress, and they had gone native now, rearing to monster height without a bloom, black and ugly as the nameless parasites that grew beside them.

*'Nature had come into her own . . .
and had encroached upon the drive
with long, tenacious fingers.'*

*'On and on, now east now west,
wound the poor thread that once had
been our drive. Sometimes I thought it
lost, but it appeared again, beneath a
fallen tree perhaps.'*

On and on, now east now west, wound the poor thread that once had been our drive. Sometimes I thought it lost, but it appeared again, beneath a fallen tree perhaps, or struggling on the other side of a muddied ditch created by the winter rains. I had not thought the way so long. Surely the miles had multiplied, even as the trees had done, and this path led but to a labyrinth, some choked wilderness, and not to the house at all. I came upon it suddenly; the approach masked by the unnatural growth of a vast shrub that spread in all directions, and I stood, my heart thumping in my breast, the strange prick of tears behind my eyes.

There was Manderley, our Manderley, secretive and silent as it had always been, the grey stone shining in the moonlight of my dream, the mullioned windows reflecting the green lawns and the terrace. Time could not wreck the perfect symmetry of those walls, nor the site itself, a jewel in the hollow of a hand.

I continue to receive letters from all over the world asking me what I based the story on, and the characters, and why did I never give the heroine a name? The answer to the last question is simple: I could not think of one, and it became a challenge in technique, the easier because I was writing in the first person. I heard later from Joan Fontaine, who starred in the first film of *Rebecca* with Sir Laurence Olivier as Maxim, that Alfred Hitchcock, the director, always referred to the narrator on set as Daphne de Winter! Perhaps he was not so far from the truth.

The narrator, the 'I' of the story, is the companion to an elderly

'The terrace sloped to the lawns, and the lawns stretched to the sea, placid . . . like a lake undisturbed by wind or storm.'

lady, Mrs Van Hopper. She is whisked away from their Mediterranean retreat, the Hotel Cote d'Azur, by Maxim de Winter, the
owner of Manderley. She marries Maxim in the knowledge only
that his first wife – Rebecca – was killed in a boating tragedy (and
not that he had murdered her). The new couple come to
Manderley in early May, as I had done, with the first swallows and
bluebells and the blood-red rhododendrons in bloom.

On the approach to the house 'I' see through the mullioned
windows that the housekeeper, Mrs Danvers, has massed the staff
in the hall to be introduced to the new Mrs de Winter, and
emerging from the car, 'I' am sick to the stomach in anticipation of
being suddenly called upon to play the role of the new Mistress of
Manderley.

I can close my eyes now, and look back on it, and see myself as I must have
been, standing on the threshold of the house, a slim, awkward figure in my
stockinette dress, clutching in my sticky hands a pair of gauntlet gloves. I can
see the great stone hall, the wide doors open to the library, the Peter Lelys
and the Vandykes on the walls, the exquisite staircase leading to the
minstrels' gallery, and there, ranged one behind the other in the hall,
overflowing to the stone passages beyond, and to the dining-room, a sea of
faces, open-mouthed and curious, gazing at me as though they were the
watching crowd about the block, and I the victim with my hands behind my
back. Someone advanced from the sea of faces, someone tall and gaunt,
dressed in deep black, whose prominent cheek-bones and great, hollow eyes
gave her a skull's face, parchment-white, set on a skeleton's frame.

She came towards me, and I held out my hand, envying her for her dignity
and her composure; but when she took my hand hers was limp and heavy,
deathly cold, and it lay in mine like a lifeless thing.

'This is Mrs Danvers,' said Maxim, and she began to speak, still leaving
that dead hand in mine, her hollow eyes never leaving my eyes, so that my
own wavered and would not meet hers, and as they did so her hand moved in
mine, the life returned to it, and I was aware of a sensation of discomfort and
of shame.

Just as I had first come as a trespasser to Menabilly, so now 'I', the
narrator, am made to feel the interloper, for Manderley is the
sepulchral home of Rebecca's spirit and 'I' am but a trespasser in
time.

Jealousy is the theme, the narrator's jealousy of Maxim's first
wife, Rebecca. Once I had found some old letters written to
Tommy by the woman he had been engaged to before we met.
Innocent, irrelevant, but a personality preserved as it were in a
time capsule by letters written in the strong hand of a woman so
much more in control, so much more dynamic than me. The green-
eyed monster showed no mercy then, nor would she now.

As the narrator nervously explores, Rebecca's powerful perso-

The arrival of the de Winters at Manderley was my arrival at Milton all those years before. I can even remember seeing a maid, Parker I think her name was, standing at the top of the staircase. She became Mrs Danvers. But it was the magnificence of the great hall, the high ceiling, the panelled walls and the portraits upon them which absorbed me first.

nality seems to radiate through the house. The west wing has been preserved by Mrs Danvers as it was in Rebecca's day, only shrouded in dust sheets, frozen in time. Rebecca is everywhere . . . in the arrangement and choice of furniture, in the candlesticks on the mantlepiece, in the pictures on the walls – 'little things, meaningless and stupid in themselves, but they were there for me to see, for me to hear, for me to feel. All had belonged to Rebecca. She had chosen them, they were not mine at all.'

The past can sometimes seem so close, and that sense of fear, of furtive unrest, struggling at length to blind unreasoning panic that the past might in some manner unforeseen become a living companion. I am a child again, climbing the dark staircase of Slyfield Hall, mingling with the memories of four generations of

Fitzwilliams at Milton. Who can ever affirm or deny that the houses which have sheltered us as children, or as adults, and our predecessors too, do not have embedded in their walls, one with the dust and cobwebs, one with the overlay of fresh wallpaper and paint, the imprint of what-has-been?

Glad to escape the shadows of the past the would-be mistress of Manderley takes a walk down to the beach with Max, wearing a mackintosh picked out at random from a pile in the flower room.

'There,' said Maxim suddenly, 'take a look at that.'

We stood on a slope of a wooded hill, and the path wound away before us to a valley, by the side of a running stream. There were no dark trees here, no tangled undergrowth, but on either side of the narrow path stood azaleas and rhododendrons, not blood-coloured like the giants in the drive, but salmon, white, and gold, things of beauty and of grace, drooping their lovely, delicate

The de Winters came to Manderley in early May, as I had done, with the first swallows and bluebells and the blood-red rhododendrons.

'On either side of the path stood azaleas and rhododendrons . . . salmon, white, and gold, things of beauty and of grace.'

heads in the soft summer rain.

The air was full of their scent, sweet and heady, and it seemed to me as though their very essence had mingled with the running waters of the stream, and become one with the falling rain and the dank rich moss beneath our feet. There was no sound here but the tumbling of the little stream, and the quiet rain. When Maxim spoke, his voice was hushed too, gentle and low, as if he had no wish to break upon the silence.

'We call it the Happy Valley,' he said.

We stood quite still, not speaking, looking down upon the clear white faces of the flowers closest to us, and Maxim stooped, and picked up a fallen petal and gave it to me. It was crushed and bruised, and turning brown at the curled edge, but as I rubbed it across my hand the scent rose to me, sweet and strong, vivid as the living tree from which it came.

Then the birds began. First a blackbird, his note clear and cool above the running stream, and after a moment he had answer from his fellow hidden in the woods behind us, and soon the still air about us was made turbulent with song, pursuing us as we wandered down into the valley, and the fragrance of the white petals followed us too. It was disturbing, like an enchanted place. I had not thought it could be as beautiful as this.

The sky, now overcast and sullen, so changed from the early afternoon, and the steady insistent rain could not disturb the soft quietude of the valley; the rain and the rivulet mingled with one another, and the liquid note of the blackbird fell upon the damp air in harmony with them both. I brushed the dripping heads of azaleas as I passed, so close they grew together, bordering the path. Little drops of water fell on to my hands from the soaked petals. There were petals at my feet too, brown and sodden, bearing their scent upon them still, and a richer older scent as well, the smell of deep moss and bitter earth, the stems of bracken, and the twisted buried roots of trees. I held Maxim's hand and I had not spoken. The spell of the Happy Valley was upon me. This at last was the core of Manderley, the Manderley I would know and learn to love. The first drive was forgotten, the black, herded woods, the glaring rhododendrons, luscious and overproud. And the vast house too, the silence of that echoing hall, the uneasy stillness of the west wing, wrapped in dust-sheets. There I was an interloper, wandering in rooms that did not know me, sitting at a desk and in a chair that were not mine. Here it was different. The Happy Valley knew no trespassers. We came to the end of the path, and the flowers formed an archway above our heads. We bent down, passing underneath, and when I stood straight again, brushing the raindrops from my hair, I saw that the valley was behind us, and the azaleas, and the trees, and, as Maxim had described to me that afternoon many weeks ago in Monte Carlo, we were standing in a little narrow cove, the shingle hard and white under our feet, and the sea was breaking on the shore beyond us.

Maxim smiled down at me, watching the bewilderment on my face.

'We were standing in a little narrow cove, the shingle hard and white under our feet.'

'It's a shock, isn't it?' he said; 'no one ever expects it. The contrast is too sudden; it almost hurts.'

But, sitting down to tea on their return, it seems that not even the enchantment of Happy Valley – 'the core of Manderley' – can resist the insidious presence of Rebecca. How powerfully is the past conjured up and released upon the present when our senses are stimulated or charmed by a long-forgotten taste or smell. . .

My fingers were messy with the butter from the crumpet, and I felt in my pocket for a handkerchief. I drew it out, a tiny scrap of a thing, lace-edged. I stared at it, frowning, for it was not mine. I remembered then that Frith had picked it up from the stone floor of the hall. It must have fallen out of the pocket in the mackintosh. I turned it over in my hand. It was grubby; little bits of fluff from the pocket clung to it. It must have been in the mackintosh pocket for a long time. There was a monogram in the corner. A tall sloping R, with the letters de W interlaced. The R dwarfed the other letters, the tail of it ran down into the cambric, away from the laced edge. It was only a small handkerchief, quite a scrap of a thing. It had been rolled in a ball and put away in the pocket and forgotten.

I must have been the first person to put on that mackintosh since the handkerchief was used. She who had worn the coat then was tall, slim, broader than me about the shoulders, for I had found it big and overlong, and the sleeves had come below my wrist. Some of the buttons were missing. She had not bothered then to do it up. She had thrown it over her shoulders like a cape, or worn it loose, hanging open, her hands deep in the pockets.

There was a pink mark upon the handerchief. The mark of lip-stick. She had rubbed her lips with the handerkerchief, and then rolled it in a ball, and left it in the pocket. I wiped my fingers with the handkerchief, and as I did so I noticed that a dull scent clung about it still. A scent I recognised, a scent I knew. I shut my eyes and tried to remember. It was something elusive, something faint and fragrant that I could not name. I had breathed it before, touched it surely, that very afternoon.

And then I knew that the vanished scent upon the handkerchief was the same as the crushed white petals of the azaleas in the Happy Valley.

The spirit of Rebecca is alive in Manderley, bottled up, preserved in time, never fading, never becoming stale, and when Mrs Danvers removes the dust sheets from Rebecca's bedroom – her dressing table, her personal things, just as they had been before her 'accident' – Rebecca's suffocating presence begins to envelope the narrator's personality. 'I so identified with Rebecca that my own dull self did not exist, had never come to Manderley. I had gone back in thought and in person to the days that were gone.'

In a final attempt to assert her own personality, and prove that she can be as fine a hostess as Rebecca, she presses Maxim to revive the once annual Manderley Ball. But, at Mrs Danvers' suggestion, she chooses to model her ball-gown on a dress worn in

Just as I had first come as a trespasser to Menabilly, so now 'I', the narrator, am made to feel the interloper, the usurper of another's role.

a portrait of Caroline de Winter, a sister of Maxim's great-great-grandfather. What she cannot know is that her choice was also Rebecca's at the last Manderley Ball. She *becomes* Rebecca – and the house, as if it were conscious of its own awful destiny, seems to come alive for the occasion.

As we crossed the great hall on the way to our rooms I realised for the first time how the house lent itself to the occasion, and how beautiful the rooms were looking. Even the drawing-room, formal and cold to my consideration when we were alone, was a blaze of colour now, flowers in every corner, red roses in silver bowls on the white cloth of the supper table, the long windows open to the terrace, where, as soon as it was dusk, the fairy lights would shine. The band had stacked their instruments ready in the minstrels' gallery above the hall, and the hall itself wore a strange, waiting air; there was a warmth about it I had never known before, due to the night itself, so still and clear, to the flowers beneath the pictures, to our own laughter as we hovered on the wide stone stairs.

The old austerity had gone. Manderley had come alive in a fashion I would not have believed possible. It was not the still quiet Manderley I knew. There was a certain significance about it now that had not been before. . . I found Clarice waiting for me in my bedroom, her round face scarlet with excitement. We giggled at one another like schoolgirls, and I bade her lock my door. There was much sound of tissue paper, rustling and mysterious. We spoke to one another softly like conspirators, we walked on tiptoe. I felt like a child again on the eve of Christmas. This padding to and fro in my room with bare feet, the little furtive bursts of laughter, the stifled exclamations, reminded me of hanging up my stocking long ago. Maxim was safe in his dressing-room, and the way through was barred against him. Clarice alone was my ally and favoured friend. The dress fitted perfectly. I stood still, hardly able to restrain my impatience while Clarice hooked me up with fumbling fingers.

'It's handsome, Madam,' she kept saying, leaning back on her heels to

'The minstrels' gallery above the hall . . . I realised for the first time how the house lent itself to the occasion.'

look at me. 'It's a dress fit for the Queen of England.'

'What about under the left shoulder there,' I said, anxiously. 'That strap of mine, is it going to show?'

'No, Madam, nothing shows.'

'How is it? How do I look?' I did not wait for her answer, I twisted and turned in front of the mirror, I frowned, I smiled. I felt different already, no longer hampered by my appearance. My own dull personality was submerged at last. 'Give me the wig,' I said excitedly, 'careful, don't crush it, the curls musn't be flat. They are supposed to stand out from the face.' Clarice stood behind my shoulder, I saw her round face beyond mine in the reflection of the looking-glass, her eyes shining, her mouth a little open. I brushed my own hair sleek behind my ears. I took hold of the soft gleaming curls with trembling fingers, laughing under my breath, looking up at Clarice.

'Oh, Clarice,' I said, 'what will Mr de Winter say?'

. . . I did not recognise the face that stared at me in the glass. The eyes were larger surely, the mouth narrower, the skin white and clear? The curls stood away from the head in a little cloud. I watched this self that was not me at all and then smiled; a new, slow smile.

'Oh, Clarice!' I said. 'Oh, Clarice!' I took the skirt of my dress in my hands and curtseyed to her, the flounces sweeping the ground. She giggled excitedly, rather embarrassed, flushed though, very pleased. I paraded up and down in front of my glass watching my reflection.

'Unlock the door,' I said, 'I'm going down. Run ahead and see if they are there.' She obeyed me, still giggling, and I lifted my skirts off the ground and followed her along the corridor.

She looked back at me and beckoned. 'They've gone down,' she whispered. . .

'Make the drummer announce me,' I whispered, 'make him beat the drum, you know how they do, and then call out Miss Caroline de Winter. I want to surprise them below.' He nodded his head, he understood. My heart fluttered absurdly, and my cheeks were burning. What fun it was, what mad ridiculous childish fun! I smiled at Clarice still crouching on the corridor. I picked up my skirt in my hands. Then the sound of the drum echoed in the great hall, startling me for a moment, who had waited for it, who knew that it would come. I saw them look up surprised and bewildered from the hall below.

'Miss Caroline de Winter,' shouted the drummer.

I came forward to the head of the stairs and stood there, smiling, my hat in my hand, like the girl in the picture. I waited for the clapping and laughter that would follow as I walked slowly down the stairs. Nobody clapped, nobody moved.

They all stared at me like dumb things. Beatrice uttered a little cry and put her hand to her mouth. I went on smiling, I put one hand on the banister.

'How do you do, Mr de Winter,' I said.

Maxim had not moved. He stared up at me, his glass in his hand. There was no colour in his face. It was ashen white. I saw Frank go to him as though he would speak, but Maxim shook him off. I hesitated, one foot already on the stairs. Something was wrong, they had not understood. Why was Maxim looking like that? Why did they all stand like dummies, like people in a trance?

Then Maxim moved forward to the stairs, his eyes never leaving my face.

'What the hell do you think you are doing?' he asked. His eyes blazed in anger. His face was still ashen white.

I could not move, I went on standing there, my hand on the banister.

'It's the picture,' I said, terrified at his eyes, at his voice. 'It's the picture, the one in the gallery.'

There was a long silence. We went on staring at each other. Nobody moved in the hall. I swallowed, my hand moved to my throat. 'What is it?' I said. 'What have I done?'

If only they would not stare at me like that with dull blank faces. If only somebody would say something. When Maxim spoke again I did not recognise his voice. It was still and quiet, icy cold, not a voice I knew.

'Go and change,' he said, 'it does not matter what you put on. Find an ordinary evening frock, anything will do. Go now, before anybody comes.'

I could not speak, I went on staring at him. His eyes were the only living things in the white mask of his face.

'What are you standing there for?' he said, his voice harsh and queer. 'Didn't you hear what I said?'

I turned and ran blindly through the archway to the corridors beyond. I caught a glimpse of the astonished face of the drummer who had announced me. I brushed past him, stumbling, not looking where I went. Tears blinded my eyes. I did not know what was happening. Clarice had gone. The corridor was deserted. I looked about me stunned and stupid like a haunted thing. Then I saw that the door leading to the west wing was open wide, and that someone was standing there.

It was Mrs Danvers. I shall never forget the expression on her face, loathsome, triumphant. The face of an exulting devil. She stood there, smiling at me.

And then I ran from her, down the long narrow passage to my own room, tripping, stumbling over the flounces of my dress.

★   ★   ★

During the war, when my husband and I were living in Hythe in Kent, I received a letter from my sister, Angela.

'By the way, there is to be a sale at Menabilly. Everything to be sold up, and the house just left to fall to bits. Do you want anything?'

Did I want anything? I wanted her, my house. I wanted every stick of furniture, from the Jacobean oak to the Victorian bamboo. But what was the use? The war had come. There was no future for man, woman or child. Anyway, Menabilly was entailed. The house itself could not be sold. No, she was just a dream, and would die, as dreams die always.

But in '43 changes of plans sent me back to Cornwall, with my three children. I had not visited Menabilly since the war began. No bombs had come her way, yet she looked like a blitzed building. The shutters were not shuttered now. The panes were broken. She had been left to die.

It was easy to climb through the front windows. The house was stripped and bare. Dirty paper on the floor. Great fungus growths from the ceiling. Moisture everywhere, death and decay. I could scarcely see the soul of her for the despair. The mould was in her bones.

Odd, yet fearful, what a few years of total neglect can do to a house, as to a man, a woman. . . . Have you seen a man who has once been handsome and strong go unshaven and unkempt? Have you seen a woman lovely in her youth raddled beneath the eyes, her hair tousled and grey?

Sadder than either, more bitter and more poignant, is a lonely house.

I returned to my furnished cottage, in angry obstinate mood. Something was dying, without hope of being saved. And I would not stand it. Yet there was nothing I could do. Nothing? There was one faint, ridiculous chance in a million. . . . I telephoned my lawyer and asked him to write to the owner of Menabilly and ask him to let the house to me for a term of years. 'He won't consent for a moment,' I said. 'It's just a shot at random.'

But the shot went home. . . . A week later my lawyer came to see me.

'By the way,' he said, 'I believe you will be able to rent Menabilly. But you must treat it as a whim, you know. The place is in a fearful state. I doubt if you could do more than camp out there occasionally.'

I stared at him in amazement. 'You mean – he would consent?' I said.

'Why, yes, I gather so,' answered my lawyer.

Then it began. Not the Battle of Britain, not the attack upon the soft underbelly of Europe that my husband was helping to conduct from Africa, but my own private war to live in Menabilly by the time winter came again. . . .

'You're mad . . . you're crazy . . . you can't do it . . . there's no lighting . . . there's no water . . . there's no heating . . . you'll get no servants . . . it's impossible!'

I stood in the dining room, surrounded by a little team of experts. There was the architect, the builder, the plumber, the electrician, and my lawyer, with a ruler in his hand which he waved like a magic baton.

'I don't think it can be done. . . .' And my answer always, 'Please, please, see if it can be done.'

The creeper cut from the windows. The windows mended. The

men upon the roof mortaring the slates. The carpenter in the house, setting up the doors. The plumber in the well, measuring the water. The electrician on the ladder, wiring the walls. And the doors and windows open that had not been open for so long. The sun warming the cold dusty rooms. Fires of brushwood in the grates. And then the scrubbing of the floors that had felt neither brush nor mop for many years. Relays of charwomen, with buckets and swabs. The house alive with men and women. Where did they come from? How did it happen? The whole thing was an impossibility in wartime. Yet it did happen. And the gods were on my side. Summer turned to autumn, autumn to December. And in December came the vans of furniture; and the goods and chattels I had stored at the beginning of the war and thought never to see again were placed, like fairy things, about the rooms at Menabilly.

The madness had paid off. When Tommy came on leave for Christmas, expecting to find us squatting in camp beds with the rain pouring through the roof, he found the telephone installed, electric light in all the rooms, a hot bath waiting, and the furniture brought from store and put in just the places he would have chosen for himself. There were sprays of holly behind every picture.

'Well, I must confess, I didn't know you had it in you,' he told me.

He grew to love it as much as I did, and forever after, during his lifetime, Christmas was always the high spot of the year.

'Perhaps it's wrong,' I would think, 'to love a block of stone like

For this day, and for this night, Menabilly belongs to me and I belong to her.

The tablet in memory of Honor Harris, heroine of The King's General. *It can be seen in Tywardreath church.*

this, as one loves a person. It cannot last. It cannot endure. Perhaps it is the very insecurity of the love that makes the passion strong. Because she is not mine by right. The house is still entailed, and one day will belong to another. . .'

I would brush the thought aside. For this day, and for this night, she belongs to me and I belong to her. And at midnight, when the children were asleep, and all was hushed and still, I would sit down at the piano and look at the panelled walls, and slowly, softly, with no one there to see, the house would whisper her secrets, and the secrets would turn to stories. In those days, in some strange and eerie fashion, we were one, the house and I.

The first book that I wrote at Menabilly was *The King's General*, based on the memoirs of Honor Harris written just before she died in 1653, and largely concerning the period of the English Civil War. A tablet in her memory may still be seen to the right of the High Altar in nearby Tywardreath Church. Honor's memoirs combine with the events of the War and papers generously made available to me by the Rashleigh family, owners of Menabilly.

During the War some of the great Cornish estates changed hands as one family pitted itself against another. Jonathan Rashleigh, a supporter of the King, retained Menabilly but was ruined and his home destroyed, so that only the outer walls remained standing. In 1824 an extraordinary detail of Menabilly's history during these troubled years came to light when William Rashleigh had certain alterations made to the house, in the course of which the outer courtyard was removed, and blocked in to form kitchens and a larder.

The architect, summoned to do the work, noticed that the buttress against the north-west corner of the house served no useful purpose, and he told the masons to demolish it. This they proceeded to do, and on knocking away several of the stones they came upon a stair, leading to a small room, or cell, at the base of the buttress. Here they found the skeleton of a young man, seated on a stool, a trencher at his feet, and the skeleton was dressed in the clothes of a Cavalier, as worn during the period of the Civil War. William Rashleigh, when he was told of the discovery, gave orders for the remains to be buried with great reverence in the churchyard at Tywardreath. And because he and his family were greatly shocked at the discovery, he ordered the masons to brick up the secret room, that no one in the household should come upon it in future. The alterations of the house continued, the courtyard was blocked in, a larder built against the buttress, and the exact whereabouts of the cell remained for ever a secret held by William Rashleigh and his architect.

It is recorded that some two hundred years ago the cell was used by Jonathan Rashleigh's father for 'shipping transactions, which necessitated privacy' – a euphemism, perhaps, for piracy or smuggling? – and as a place of confinement for Jonathan's elder brother, 'who was not in full possession of his faculties . . .' Here, poor John, as the wretched man was called, would be rendered unconscious due to lack of air and close confinement, the more easy then to handle. This is how Honor Harris describes the cell in 1646: 'Six foot high, four square, it was not larger than a closet, and the stone walls, clammy cold with years, icy to my touch. There was a little stool against the corner, and by its side an empty trencher, with a wooden spoon. Cobwebs and mould were thick upon them, and I thought of the last meal that had been eaten

Menabilly, looking across the roofs to where the buttress once stood. When they demolished it they found the skeleton of a young man, seated on a stool, a trencher at his feet, and the skeleton was dressed in the clothes of a Cavalier, as worn during the period of the Civil War.

'Richard's callous attitude to prisoners – dumped within Lydford Castle and hanged without trial – showed me that streak of cruelty I had always known was in his nature.'

there, a quarter of a century before, by idiot uncle John.' And the unfortunate Cavalier? William Rashleigh learnt that certain members of the Grenville family had hidden at Menabilly before the Cornish rising of 1648, and he surmised that one of them had taken refuge in the secret room and had been forgotten.

There are no more Grenvilles. One of the proudest and most famous families amongst the Cornish gentry is extinct in Cornwall, the name passing to other branches east of the Tamar. Richard Grenville and his brother Bevil were key figures in the Royalist cause during the Civil War. Their grandfather, Sir Richard Grenville, had died holding off fifty-two Spanish galleons from the deck of his small ship *Revenge*. Lion-hearted courage was a quality inherited by both grandsons, but it was to Richard – the King's General of the novel – that the great man bequeathed his characteristic ruthlessness.

'It is a splendid sign,' says his nephew Jack in the novel, 'when my uncle gives vent to frowns and curses. It mostly means he is well pleased. But see him smile, and speak with courtesy, and you may well reckon that the luckless receiver of his favours is half-way to the guardroom. I once saw him curse a fellow for fifteen minutes without respite, and that evening promote him to the rank of Captain. The next day he received a prisoner, a country squire, I think, from Barnstaple, who owed him money, and my uncle plied

Above: *Castle Dor, where 'the guns and foot of a Parliament Army capitulated to King Charles on his last campaign of the West.'*

Right: *The curious and the nostalgic, desiring to wander where the Grenvilles once rode, hawked and hunted, can first drive to Kilkhampton church and look upon their sculptured monuments, then turn coastward towards Coombe, where the fine old farmhouse of Stowe Barton stands above the site of the two Grenville houses.*

him with wine, and smiles, and favours. He was hanging from a tree at Buckland two hours afterwards.'

Honor Harris and Richard Grenville are thrown together by the marriage of Honor's brother Kit to Richard's beautiful, but poisonous sister, Gartred. Despite the opposition of her mother to the match (and her own reason), Honor falls in love. As they court secretly in the orchard of the Harris home at Lanrest, Honor surprises a gentleness in Richard and, 'too much in love to care a whit for anyone', they decide to get married. But when out hawking near the Grenville estate at Stowe in North Cornwall, Honor is thrown from her horse:

We rode out to the open country, with the wind blowing in our faces and the sound of the Atlantic coming to us as the long surf rollers spilt themselves with a roar on to the shore far below. At first the sport was poor, for no quarry larger than a woodcock was flushed, and to this the goshawks were flown, who clutch their prey between their claws, and do not kill outright, like the large-winged peregrines. Richard's falcon and Gartred's tiercel were still hooded, and not slipped, for we were not yet come upon the heron's feeding ground. My little mare pawed restlessly at the ground, for up to the present we had had no run and the pace was slow. Near a little copse the falconers flushed three magpies and a cast of goshawks were flown at them, but the cunning magpies, making up for lack of wing power by cunning, scuttled from hedge to hedge, and after some twenty minutes or so of hovering by the hawks, and shouting and driving by the falconers, only one magpie was taken.

'Come. This is poor indeed,' said Gartred scornfully. 'Can we find no

'Near a little copse the falconers flushed three magpies.'

better quarry, and so let fly the falcons?'

Richard shaded his eyes from the sun, and looked towards the west. A long strip of moorland lay before us, rough and uneven, and at the far end of it a narrow, soggy marsh, where the duck would fly to feed in stormy weather, and at all seasons of the year, so Richard told me, the sea-birds came, curlews, and gulls, and herons.

There was no bird as yet on passage through the sky, save a small lark high above our heads, and the marsh, where the herons might be found, was still two miles away.

'I'll match my horse to yours, and my red hawk to your tiercel,' said Richard suddenly, and even as he spoke he let fly the hood of his falcon and slipped her, putting spurs to his horse upon the gesture. Within ten seconds Gartred had followed suit, her grey-winged peregrine soaring into the sun, and she and Richard were galloping across the moors towards the marsh, with the two hawks like black specks in the sky above them. My mare, excited by the clattering hoofs of her companions, took charge of me, nearly pulling my arms out of their sockets, and she raced like a mad thing in pursuit of the horses ahead of us, the yelping of the dogs and the cries of the falconers whipping her speed. My last ride. The sun in my eyes, the wind in my face, the movement of the mare beneath me, the thunder of her hooves, the scent of the golden gorse, the sound of the sea. Unforgettable, unforgotten, deep in my soul for all time. I could see Richard and Gartred racing neck to neck, flinging insults at each other as they rode, and in the sky

'Richard shaded his eyes from the sun, and looked towards the west. A long strip of moorland lay before us, rough and uneven . . . "Beware the chasm," Richard shouted in my ear.'

the male and female falcons pitched and hovered. When suddenly away from the marsh ahead of us rose a heron, his great grey wings unfolding, his legs trailing. I heard a shout from Richard, and an answering cry from Gartred, and an instant it seemed the hawks had seen their quarry, for they both began to circle above the heron, climbing higher and still higher, swinging out in rings until they were like black dots against the sun. The watchful heron, rising too, but in a narrower circle, turned down-wind, his queer, ungainly body strangely light and supple, and like a flash the first hawk dived to him – whether it was Richard's young falcon or Gartred's tiercel I could not tell – and missed the heron by a hair's breadth. At once, recovering himself, he began to soar again, in ever higher circles, to recover his lost pitch, and the second hawk swooped, missing in like manner.

I tried to rein in my mare, but could not stop her, and now Gartred and Richard had turned eastward too, following the course of the heron, and we were galloping three abreast, the ground rising steadily towards a circle of stones in the midst of the moor.

'Beware the chasm,' shouted Richard in my ear, pointing with his whip, but he was past me like the wind and I could not call to him.

The heron was now direct above my head, and the falcons lost to view, and I heard Gartred shout in triumph: 'They bind – they bind – my tiercel has her,' and, silhouetted against the sun, I saw one of the falcons locked against the heron and two come swinging down to earth not twenty yards ahead.

I tried to swerve, but the mare had the mastery, and I shouted to Gartred as she passed me, 'Which way is the chasm?' but she did not answer me. On we flew towards the circle of stones, the sun blinding my eyes, and out of the darkening sky fell the dying heron and the blood-bespattered falcon, straight into the yawning crevice that opened out before me. I heard Richard shout, and a thousand voices singing in my ears as I fell.

It was thus, then, that I, Honor Harris of Lanrest, became a cripple, losing all power in my legs from that day forward until this day on which I write, so that for some twenty-five years now, I have been upon my back, or upright in a chair, never walking any more, or feeling the ground beneath my feet. If anyone therefore thinks that a cripple makes an indifferent heroine to a tale, now is the time to close these pages and desist from reading. For you will never see me wed to the man I love, nor become the mother of his children. But you will learn how that love never faltered, for all its strange viscissitudes, becoming to both of us, in later years, more deep and tender than if we had been wed, and you will learn also how, for all my helplessness, I took the leading part in the drama that unfolded, my very immobility sharpening my senses and quickening my perception, while chance itself forced me to my role of judge and witness. The play goes on, then – what you have just read is but the prologue.

As in *Rebecca*, I identified strongly with the narrator. As the drama unfolds Honor Harris becomes an extension of the author, my persona in the past. And when the fate of the young Cavalier – Richard Grenville's son – is sealed, I feel the shadow of the buttress is upon both Honor and me. Sitting at my typewriter only yards from the site of the airless room I too hear 'the sound of a boy's

As I sat before my typewriter, only yards from the buttress cell, I felt like the crippled heroine of the novel, constrained, frustrated from participating, an invalid of time.

voice calling my name in terror, of a boy's hand beating against the walls', and in the pitch-black night, I fancy I can see his ghost, 'vivid, terrible, accusing'. Then, like the crippled heroine of my novel, I feel constrained, frustrated at participating in the events of yesterday merely as 'judge and witness', an invalid of time.

★   ★   ★

The third of my novels set largely at Menabilly is *My Cousin Rachel*. It tells the story of Philip Ashley whose cousin and legal guardian, Ambrose, marries the equivocal Rachel who lives in Florence. It is Rachel's second marriage; her first husband – an Italian named Sangaletti – having been killed in a duel. Philip receives two letters from Ambrose after the marriage, which appear to indicate that Rachel is poisoning him. Soon afterwards, Ambrose dies.

Real history is not exhumed in the way that it is in *The King's General*, from old manuscripts and family papers, although in another century there really was a Philip who was related to a Rachel, who was married to an Ambrose. Indeed if you go to Florence and drive towards Fiesole you might find Rachel's villa – but not under the name of Sangaletti! There is even a portrait of Rachel, although I have never seen it. I am told it is most compelling – her dark eyes follow you about the room. That fact alone, learned during a visit to Italy, seemed to me good enough to start a story brewing!

My Cousin Rachel, motivated by the twin demons jealousy and suspicion, turns on the way the past can and does re-surface in the present, and it does so in the novel by means of letters. Letters set the tale in motion, they hint of conspiracy and act as an anchor of truth in shifting sands of self-deception. But there are also letters that are never sent or are mislaid, which appear long after they have been written to haunt those who would write their own scripts of what-has-been for their own self-serving ends.

Philip himself owes much to Eric Avon, a splendid character I invented for myself in early adolescence in response to the pressure on one at the time to have an idol or 'crush'. Kisses 'by hopeless fancy feigned on lips that are for others' were not really in my line, not at thirteen, so I invented Eric, a kind of safe, English public school hero who undoubtedly owed much to my early tea-time reading of *Tom Brown's Schooldays*, *The Fifth Form at St Dominics*, *Teddy Lester's Schooldays*, and watching the annual Eton v. Harrow cricket match at Lord's. Eric re-emerged in different guises as the narrator of five novels I was to write at long intervals, in the first person, masculine gender: *I'll Never Be Young Again*, *My Cousin Rachel*, *The Scapegoat*, *The Flight of the Falcon*, and *The House on the Strand*. None resembled Eric very closely, but like him all five personalities can be seen to be undeveloped, inadequate in some way.

Philip and his guardian Ambrose live together at Menabilly in a kind of gentlemanly misogyny through Philip's boyhood, adolescence and early manhood, and when Ambrose meets and marries Rachel while on holiday in Italy, Philip feels an enormous sense of loss, and not a little jealous.

On Ambrose's death Philip adopts the role of investigator, and with characteristic, mock-heroic courage he travels to Italy to confront Rachel with the evidence of Ambrose's two letters which appear to suggest foul play. When he arrives in Florence, Rachel has disappeared, and her smooth-talking advisor, Rainaldi (the absolute antithesis of the ingenue, Philip) does little to dispel the young man's suspicions.

The official death certificate shows that Ambrose died of a brain tumour, and on Philip's return to Menabilly his godfather, Nick Kendall, informs him that there is a family susceptibility to cerebral disease which would seem to corroborate the autopsy. Philip, however, remains unconvinced.

When Rachel decides to return from Italy to her native Cornwall she writes to Philip to ask whether she might bring home her late husband's effects and stay a while at Menabilly, of which she has heard so much from Ambrose. Unable to voice sound grounds of refusal, Philip agrees but decides to act coldly towards her so that her stay will at least be as short as possible.

However, within days of their meeting, Philip finds himself hopelessly in love. It is an odd, almost child-like infatuation,

Philip shows his cousin Rachel around the Menabilly estate: 'The Barton farm, and the house itself – the mansion, as Seecombe always called it – lay in a sort of saucer.'

'The shocks of corn were golden in the last rays of the sun.'

unquestioning, adoring, the son looking for his mother. And Philip pursues his quarry with boyish enthusiasm, consigning his suspicions about Rachel and Rainaldi's role in the death of his guardian to the back of his mind. Not that he finds this easy; intimations of the dark side of Rachel's character appear to be everywhere – she is anxious on hearing that he had visited Florence and met Rainaldi; Philip finds a telling scrap of a letter from Ambrose when unpacking an old trunk that Rachel has brought from Italy; there is a suggestion that Rachel has been reckless with money, and when Philip supplies her with money it appears that she is sending it to Italy.

Then, one fine Spring morning, Philip is called to Sam Bate's house, the Lodge on the east boundary of Menabilly.

The old driveway to the lodge. 'In the afternoon I walked up the avenue to the gates where the four roads meet, and turned in at the lodge.'

Blackbird and chaffinch sang beneath our window on first waking, rousing both Rachel and myself from sleep. We talked of it at midday when we met. The sun came to her first, on the eastern side of the house, and with her windows wide drove a slant of light on to her pillow. I had it later, as I dressed. Leaning out, looking over the meadows to the sea, I would see the horses and the plough climb the further hill, with the gulls wheeling about them, and in the pasture lands closer to the house were the ewes and the young lambs, back to back for comfort. Lapwings, on passage bent, came in a little cloud, with fluttering wings. Soon they would pair, and the male soar and tumble in his flight of rapture. Down on the shore the curlews whistled, and the oyster-catchers, black and white like parsons, poked in the seaweed solemnly, for breakfast. The air had a zest to it, salt-tasting, under the sun.

It was on a morning such as this that Seecombe came to me and told me that Sam Bate, up at the East Lodge, who was in bed, poorly, wished very much that I would go and see him, as he had something of importance to give me. He implied that whatever it was he had was too precious to deliver to his son or to his daughter. I thought little of it. It is always a pleasure amongst country folk to make much mystery over small matters. Nevertheless, in the afternoon, I walked up the avenue to the gates there where the four roads meet, and turned in at the lodge to have a word with him. Sam was sitting up in bed, and lying on the blanket before him was one of the coats that had belonged to Ambrose, which had been given to him on Christmas Day. I recognised it as the light-coloured one I had not known, which Ambrose must have bought for the hot weather on the continent.

Sam explains that he has found a letter lodged between the material of the coat and the lining: 'It shook me, sir, to come upon it. It seemed, if you understand, as though I had come upon a message from the dead.' Sam gives the letter, still un-opened, to Philip, who thanks him and takes his leave.

I did not return at once to the house. I climbed up through the woods to a path that runs above that part of the estate, bordering the Trenant acres and the wooded avenue. Ambrose had been fonder of this walk than any other. It was our highest point of land, saving the beacon to the south, and had a fine view over the woods and the valley to the open sea. The trees fringing the path, planted by Ambrose and his father before him, gave shelter, although not high enough as yet to dim the view, and in May month the bluebells made a cover to the ground. At the end of the path, topping the woods, before plunging to descent and the keeper's cottage in the gully, Ambrose had set up a piece of granite. 'This,' he said to me, half joking, half in earnest, 'can serve me for tombstone when I die. Think of me here, rather than in the family

'It was our highest point of land, saving the beacon to the south, and had a fine view over the woods and the valley to the open sea.'

vault with the other Ashleys.'

I sat down beside the slab, and taking Ambrose's letter from my pocket placed it face downwards, on my knee. The red seal stared up at me, imprinted with his ring and the chough's head. The packet was not thick. It contained nothing. Nothing but a letter, which I did not want to open. I cannot say what misgiving held me back, what cowardly instinct drove me to hide my head like an ostrich in the sand. Ambrose was dead, and the past went with him when he died. I had my own life to make, and my own will to follow.

But not to read the letter . . . what would he say to that? If I tore it now to shreds, and scattered the pieces, and never learnt the contents, would he condemn me? I balanced the letter in my hand, this way and that. To read, or not to read; I wished to heaven the choice was not before me. Back in the house, my loyalty was with her. In the boudoir, with my eyes upon her face, watching those hands, that smile, hearing her voice, no letter would have haunted me. Yet here, in the woods beside the slab of granite where we had so often stood together, he and I, Ambrose holding the very stick I carried now, wearing the same coat, here his power was strongest. Like a small boy who prays that the weather shall be fine upon his birthday I prayed God now that the letter should contain nothing to disturb me, and so opened it. It was dated April of the preceding year, and was therefore written three months before he died.

Dearest boy,

If my letters have been infrequent, it is not because I have not thought of you. You have been in my mind, these past months, perhaps more than ever before. But a letter can miscarry, or be read by others, and I would not wish either of those things to happen; therefore I have not written, or when I have done so I know there has been little in anything I have said. I have been ill, with fever and a bad headache. Better now. But for how long, I cannot tell. The fever may come again, and the headaches too, and when in the grip of them I am not responsible for what I say or do. This much is certain.

But I am not yet certain of the cause. Philip, dear boy, I am much disturbed. That is lightly said. I am in agony of mind. I wrote to you, during the winter I think it was, but was ill shortly afterwards and have no recollection what happened to the letter, I may very well have destroyed it in the mood that possessed me. . .

As the months passed I noticed more and more how she turned to this man I have mentioned before in my letters, signor Rainaldi, a friend and I gather a lawyer of Sangalletti's, for advice, rather than to me. I believe this man to have a pernicious influence upon her. I suspect him of having been in love with her for years, even when Sangalletti was alive, and although I do not for an instant believe that she ever thought of him in such a connexion up to a short while ago, now, since she has altered in her manner to me, I cannot be so sure. There is a shadow in her eye, a tone in her voice, when this name is said, that awakens in my mind the most terrible suspicion. . .

At times she seems like her true self, and all is well, so well that I feel

'Think of me here, rather than in the family vault with the other Ashleys.'

I have been through some nightmare and wake again to the happiness of the first months of our marriage. Then, with a word or an action, all is lost again. I will come down to the terrace and find Rainaldi there. At sight of me, both fall silent. I cannot but wonder what it is they have been discussing. Once, when she had gone into the villa and Rainaldi and I were alone, he asked an abrupt question as to my will. This he had seen, incidentally, when we married. He told me that as it stood, and should I die, I would leave my wife without provision. This I knew, and had anyway drawn up a will myself that would correct the error, and would have put my signature to it, and had it witnessed, could I be certain that her fault of spending was a temporary passing thing, and not deep-rooted.

This new will, by the way, would give her the house, and the estate for her lifetime only, and so to you upon her death, with the proviso that the running of the estate be left in your hands entirely.

It still remains unsigned, and for the reason I have told you.

Mark you, it is Rainaldi who asked questions on the will, Rainaldi who drew my attention to the omissions of the one that stands at present. She does not speak of it, to me. But do they speak of it together? What is it that they say to one another, when I am not there?

This matter of the will occurred in March. Admittedly, I was unwell, and nearly blinded with my head, and Rainaldi bringing up the matter may have done so in that cold calculating way of his, thinking that I might die. Possibly it is so. Possibly it is not discussed between them. I have no means of finding out. Too often now I find her eyes upon me, watchful and strange. And when I hold her, it is as though she were afraid. Afraid of what, of whom?

Two days ago, which brings me to the reason for this letter, I had another attack of this same fever, which laid me low in March. The onset is sudden. I am seized with pains and sickness, which passes swiftly to great excitation of my brain, driving me near to violence, and I can hardly stand upon my feet for dizziness of mind and body. This, in its turn, passes, and an intolerable desire for sleep comes upon me, so that I fall upon the floor, or upon my bed, with no power over my limbs. I do not recollect my father being thus. The headaches, yes, and some difficulty of temperament, but not the other symptoms.

Philip, my boy, the only being in the world whom I can trust, tell me what it means, and if you can, come out to me. Say nothing to Nick Kendall. Say no word to any single soul. Above all, write not a word in answer, merely come.

One thought possesses me, leaving me no peace. Are they trying to poison me?

Ambrose

I folded the letter back into its creases. The dog stopped barking in the cottage garden below. I heard the keeper open his gate and the dog yelp at him in welcome. I heard voices from the cottage, the clank of a pail, the shutting of a door. From the trees on the hill opposite the jackdaws rose in flight, and circled, cawing, and moved in a black cloud to the tops of the other trees, beside the marshes.

I did not tear the letter. I dug a hole for it, beneath the slab of granite. I put it inside my pocket-book, and buried the pocket-book, deep in the dark earth. Then I smoothed the place with my hands. I walked away down the hill, and through the woods to the avenue below. As I climbed again, up the back way to the house, I heard the laughter and the chatter of the men as they went home from work. I stood a moment and watched them trudge off across the park. The scaffolding placed against the walls where they had been working all the day looked bleak and bare.

Later Philip suffers a sudden, unexplained illness and the floodgates of suspicion open wide once more, and when recovered, he follows Rachel to Fowey and witnesses a clandestine meeting with Rainaldi. At night Philip dreams of the granite stone and he goes to disinter Ambrose's letter, reading his words afresh as a warning for himself. He tears and scatters it upon the field, and then returns to Menabilly to find a letter from Rainaldi waiting for Rachel. Searching Rachel's room for evidence of a conspiracy he discovers an envelope of laburnum seeds and remembers that he

The gibbet at Four Turnings.

'"There you are, Philip," Ambrose said . . . "There's no escape. You can't learn the lesson too young. This is how a felon dies."

"Tom had a bright face when I saw him last," I answered. "Now he isn't fresh enough to become bait for his own lobsters."'

had seen a laburnum tree at Rachel's home in Florence – could the seeds have been used to poison him, and Ambrose before him?

When Rachel announces that she wishes to take a walk to the sunken garden in the grounds of Menabilly, Philip deliberately refrains from warning her that the bridge she must cross has been left unsupported while under construction. But as Rachel walks to her death, seeds of other herbs are discovered, quite innocent; Rainaldi's letter, when opened and read, is non-committal; Philip finds a drawing of Ambrose with an invocation only to remember the good times. . . As Rachel dies her would-be suitor's grounds for suspicion seem to evaporate into the still Spring air.

I have often been asked whether Rachel was really guilty of murdering Ambrose or whether it was all in Philip's mind. And I have to say that my characters, once their personalities are formed, defy intervention by their author. In *My Cousin Rachel* I am the narrator, Philip, and quite genuinely I cannot answer the question whether Rachel was a poisoner. One moment I thought, 'Well, I wonder if she is?' and the next moment I was not at all sure. So it's left like that in the book for the reader – like Philip – to wonder.

What is certain is that our past will not be buried, for it is alive, with us and within us. Philip's head-in-the-sand attitude serves only to expose the futility of trying to escape the hours and the days. Yesterday is not some milestone that has been passed in the journey of life, to be forgotten, buried. Like the ancient places and buildings around us, we are other than we were because of yesterday. And the past is intrinsic to our future, our destiny. This, Philip will undoubtedly discover, for from the opening pages of *My Cousin Rachel*, the hangman's gibbet, which once stood at Four Turnings near the east lodge at Menabilly, is a kind of symbol of Philip's fate, insinuating, illuminating, rolling past, present and future into one. Four Turnings is the place where all roads meet, and where all strands of Philip's story seem to converge. Now, in his present crisis, the burden of guilt laying heavy on his shoulders, Philip's mind returns to the day when, as a young boy, he saw Tom Jenkyn hanging there lifeless in his chains, and he fears that their destinies may always have been linked. 'He killed his wife, so Ambrose said. And that was all.'

CHAPTER FIVE

THINGS UNKNOWN

~

There is a faculty amongst the myriad threads of our inheritance that, unlike the chemicals in our bodies and in our brains, has not yet been pinpointed by science, or even fully examined. I like to call this faculty 'the sixth sense'. It is a sort of seeing, a sort of hearing, something between perception and intuition, an indefinable grasp of things unknown.

I have always been fascinated by psychic matters although I'm not psychic myself – I've never met a ghost and don't care to contact 'the other world' or anything of that sort. But I do think there is something in what they call ESP, extra-sensory perception.

The phenomena of precognition, of telepathy, of dreaming true, all depend upon the sixth sense, and the therapeutic value of hypnosis, still in its infancy, depends upon it too. Latent in young children, animals and primitive peoples, and more highly developed in the East than in the West, this perceptual intuitive sense has long lain dormant in most civilised societies and is waiting to be tapped.

Many of my short stories, even the early ones like *The Apple Tree*, have a sort of psychic dimension. And of course the phenomenon appears in my story *Don't Look Now*, which became a wonderful film with Donald Sutherland and Julie Christie. The story was triggered in my mind by a visit to Venice. There are a lot of rather frightening little alleys, bridges and streets near the narrow canals before you come to Saint Marco. Walking there one night I saw what looked like a little child, running beside a side canal and I thought, this is sinister. The story is very spooky, but then Venice is spooky if you go out at night and walk around the back streets. The hero of the story, John, presages his own funeral but resists his knowledge and pours scorn on the psychic relationship which develops between his wife and two elderly sisters whom they meet in Venice. Only at the moment of his own death at the hands of a hideous red-coated dwarf (whom he had taken to be a child in distress) does John realise how blind he has been.

The sixth sense is a sort of seeing, a sort of hearing, something between perception and intuition, an indefinable grasp of things unknown. It is a power which links man with the Infinite and the Eternal.

In a short story called *The Breakthrough* I explored the exciting possibilities in psychic communication between individuals, and between people and animals. Only a lover of animals will understand the intuitive bond of communication that exists, say, between a person and his dog. *The Breakthrough* goes further and suggests that the force which enables this form of telepathy, indeed all the psychic mysteries, is the life-force which survives us after death. In ignoring this power we have all too readily cut ourselves off from our fellows in nature from whom we would do well to

learn, and widened the gulf between ourselves and God.

If anything deepens belief in a Creator it is by watching wildlife in the countryside, a constant miracle, and noting the changes in their routine through the seasons; something that applies equally to the colour and growth of trees, plants and shrubs, even weeds. All are bound to natural law, which is surely God's law. One of the greatest miracles of all is the migration of swallows. The first week in May I stand in my small front garden and wait and watch. They never fail to arrive, and I wave, 'Hurrah, and welcome!' as they make for my roof, or the old nest inside my garage that was their home the preceding year. Here they rear their young, generally two broods, and by September they begin to prepare for Autumn flight. They fly overhead in a restless manner. 'Safe journey, and a good winter!' I call. The following day they have gone. They are obeying natural law.

Alfred Hitchcock bought the film rights to The Birds *after his success with* Jamaica Inn *and* Rebecca. *But he set it in America when it was meant to have happened at Menabilly Barton Farm. I walked down to the farm one day and saw the farmer on his tractor with all the gulls overhead and thought, supposing they attacked!*

Walking down from Menabilly to the farm one day, I caught sight of the farmer on his tractor ploughing his fields, a cloud of screaming gulls circling above his head, and thought, 'Supposing the gulls attacked!' That picture started the brewing process for my short story, *The Birds*.

The birds had been more restless than ever this fall of the year, the agitation more marked because the days were still. As the tractor traced its path up and down the western hills, the figure of the farmer silhouetted on the driving-seat, the whole machine and the man upon it would be lost momentarily in the great cloud of wheeling, crying birds. There were many more than usual, Nat was sure of this. Always, in autumn, they followed the plough, but not in great flocks like these, nor with such clamour.

Nat remarked upon it, when hedging was finished for the day. 'Yes,' said the farmer, 'there are more birds about than usual; I've noticed it too. And daring, some of them, taking no notice of the tractor. One or two gulls came so close to my head this afternoon I thought they'd knock my cap off! As it was, I could scarcely see what I was doing, when they were overhead and I had the sun in my eyes. I have a notion the weather will change. It will be a hard winter. That's why the birds are restless.'

Nat, tramping home across the fields and down the lane to his cottage, saw the birds still flocking over the western hills, in the last glow of the sun. No wind, and the grey sea calm and full. Campion in bloom yet in the hedges, and the air mild. The farmer was right, though, and it was that night the weather turned. Nat's bedroom faced east. He woke up just after after two and heard the wind in the chimney. Not the storm and bluster of a sou'westerly gale, bringing the rain, but east wind, cold and dry. It sounded hollow in the chimney, and a loose slate rattled on the roof. Nat listened, and he could hear the sea roaring in the bay. Even the air in the small bedroom had turned chill: a draught came under the skirting of the door, blowing upon the bed. Nat drew the blanket round him, leant closer to the back of his sleeping wife, and stayed wakeful, watchful, aware of misgiving without cause.

Then he heard the tapping on the window. There was no creeper on the cottage walls to break loose and scratch upon the pane. He listened, and the tapping continued until, irritated by the sound, Nat got out of bed and went to the window. He opened it, and as he did so something brushed his hand, jabbing at his knuckles, grazing the skin. Then he saw the flutter of the wings and it was gone, over the roof, behind the cottage.

In the story, the gulls act as one body, bound together by some extra-ordinary power against a human prey so 'civilised' that few can understand, can recognise that in some sinister way the evolutionary tide has turned.

He lifted his face to the sky. It was colourless and grey. The bare trees on the landscape looked bent and blackened by the east wind. The cold did not affect the living birds, waiting out there in the fields.

'This is the time they ought to get them,' said Nat, 'they're a sitting target now. They must be doing this all over the country. Why don't our aircraft take off now and spray them with mustard gas? What are all our chaps doing? They must know, they must see for themselves. . .'

As he jumped the stile he heard the whirr of wings. A black-backed gull dived down at him from the sky, missed, swerved in flight, and rose to dive again. In a moment it was joined by others, six, seven, a dozen, black-backed and herring mixed. Nat dropped his hoe. The hoe was useless. Covering his head with his arms he ran towards the cottage. They kept on coming at him from the air, silent save for the beating wings. The terrible, fluttering wings. He could feel the blood on his hands, his wrists, his neck. Each stab of a swooping beak tore his flesh. If only he could keep them from his eyes. Nothing else mattered. He must keep them from his eyes. They had not learnt yet how to cling to a shoulder, how to rip clothing, how to dive in mass upon the head, upon the body. But with each dive, with each attack, they became bolder. And they had no thought for themselves. When they dived low and missed, they crashed, bruised and broken, on the ground. As Nat ran he stumbled, kicking their spent bodies in front of him.

He found the door, he hammered upon it with his bleeding hands. Because of the boarded windows no light shone. Everything was dark.

'Let me in,' he shouted, 'it's Nat. Let me in.'

He shouted loud to make himself heard above the whirr of the gulls' wings.

Then he saw the gannet, poised for the dive, above him in the sky. The gulls circled, retired, soared, one with another, against the wind. Only the gannet remained. One single gannet, above him in the sky. The wings folded suddenly to its body. It dropped like a stone. Nat screamed, and the door opened. He stumbled across the threshold, and his wife threw her weight against the door.

They heard the thud of the gannet as it fell.

This extra-ordinary source of power, this strange and sometimes mystical sense can act as guide, as mentor, warning us of danger, signalling caution, but it can also urge us to new discoveries and intuitions. Perhaps it explains my instinctual desire to recapture the past – a past often tantalizingly out of reach of our so-called normal senses. Certainly I believe the desire to belong both to the past and the present goes very deep in human nature, and it is an urge that strengthens when we get older.

My Grandpapa George developed the ability to 'visit' the past by dreaming true. He would lie back and in his mind's eye become the child he once was, and he wrote about this 'psychic' ability too. George, who was never known as George but as Kicky, a nickname which he carried to the end of his days, was the eldest of three children born, in Paris in 1834, of Louis-Maturin Busson du Maurier and Ellen Clarke, the daughter of the notorious Mary Anne Clarke, whose liaison with the Duke of York at the beginning of the nineteenth century caused so much scandal and who was the

My grandfather, George du Maurier, who explored the 'vast, mysterious power, latent in the sub-conscious of man' in his novel, Peter Ibbetson.

subject of my novel, *Mary Anne*. She was a very lively lady.

When he came to London, he had nothing. But in 1865, when John Leech – the well-known illustrator of *Punch* magazine – died, his mantle fell on George's shoulders; he was only thirty-one years old. In those days *Punch* magazine stood alone, the only weekly paper of its kind. A gibe at the government from *Punch* in 1870, and worried members of Parliament would be discussing the fact in the lobbies the same day. Only the best draughtsmen of the day contributed to *Punch*, and with them the wittiest writers, the ablest critics. Had George ended his days as a draughtsman only, he would long have been remembered and loved for this work alone.

Despite his early fame, George looked upon his early life in Paris with deep nostalgia and almost passionate regret, as though in the depths of him there was a seed of melancholy, a creature unfulfilled. The happy memory of childhood was a memory he clung to all his life, and his wistful longing for what-was-once and cannot-be-again came to the surface in the written word when, in 1891, he published his first novel, *Peter Ibbetson*. It was enormously popular in its day, and George became a very rich man.

In the novel, Peter Ibbetson has an idyllic childhood in Paris and develops a wonderful friendship with a little girl called Mary, with whom he constructs a mythical 'Peter Pan' world with its own private language. At the moment of true happiness, Peter is ophaned and sent to England, and his friendship with Mary is curtailed.

In the artificial High Society world in which he finds himself, Peter develops a growing sense of ennui and dissillusionment. In an effort to find consolation he turns to the arts, and music becomes a powerful force in his life, as indeed it did for George who worshipped beauty and was not ashamed to put his ideals upon paper. This was something that George's generation understood, for to many of his contemporaries, beauty was an end in itself, and to George himself no emotion could be compared with that felt by a sensitive person on hearing a well-trained voice or violin.

At this point in the life of his fictional creation, Peter falls in love with a woman called Mme Serakier, who turns out to be the girlfriend from his childhood. With her help Peter develops the sixth sense which permits him access to the longed for idyll of his childhood. Mary tells Peter that she learned to develop the ability from her father: 'My dear father had learned a strange secret of the brain – how in sleep to recall past things and people and places as they had once been seen and known by him – even unremembered things. He called it "dreaming true", and by long practice, he told me, he had brought the art of doing this to perfection. . . . Thus have I revisited in sleep every place I have ever lived in, and especially this the beloved spot where I first as a girl knew you!'

With Mary's help, Peter becomes a master at dreaming true and develops an awareness of 'a dim sense of some vast mysterious power, latent in the sub-conscious of man – unheard of, un-dreamed of as yet, but linking him with the Infinite and the Eternal.'

My novel *The House on the Strand* owes a great debt to Grandpapa George and his Peter Ibbetson. I think he affected all of us children greatly. But its inspiration needed a vehicle, a storyline, which did not emerge until 1964, the year that Tommy and I realised that our lease at Menabilly was coming to an end and that we would have to look for another home.

The thought of moving from this particular bit of Cornwall was unbearable to both of us. But then, like a miracle, the lease of the one-time dower house to Menabilly – Kilmarth – fell vacant, and it was only half a mile or so away, with a splendid view over the sea beloved so well.

Moving house after twenty-six years, is rather like facing a major

Kilmarth, the one-time dower house to Menabilly, to which I moved in 1969.

I would miss the acres of woodland that surround Menabilly, but Kilmarth has a splendid view over the sea, beloved so well.

Ygdrasil, *the little boat in which Tommy had come down to Fowey. She really was terrific in those days, way back in 1932, big cockpit, twin engines in the stern, beautifully decorated inside, pictures all round; she really was a fine sight. Now she, or what's left of her, sits in my garden at Kilmarth.*

operation. Especially if the house one leaves behind has been greatly loved. Also I felt sorry for the house; I was sure it would be melancholy without us.

There is a plant, the mandrake, which bleeds and shrieks when it is pulled up, and that is how I felt on leaving Menabilly. The feeling passed, but it was nearly ten years before I finally laid the ghost. I hadn't been back inside Menabilly since leaving her (though to be truthful, I had taken to trespassing in the grounds again), and then one day I heard someone wasn't well and decided to take some apples over. I was invited inside. I hesitated, but went in, and looked around. You know, when I got back here, I remembered it not the way it was that morning, but the way it had been when she was mine.

I moved to Kilmarth in June, 1969. Day by day, week by week, month by month, during the run-up period when we were planning what we hoped would be our final home, I would visit the empty house and walk round the rooms in a daze, trying to picture the sort of people who had lived in the house before. I found a lot of dusty bottles in a room in the basement, bottles containing curious things like embryos. My predecessor had been a scientist, Professor Singer, I began to imagine what he got up to in this old house. . .

Tommy organised everything, even to writing out the labels for the removal man and deciding where the furniture should go. And he signed the lease a few weeks before he died. Death to the novelist is a familiar theme. Often it is the high spot of a particular tale, turning romance to tragedy. It is only when death touches the

Tommy signed the lease to Kilmarth a few weeks before he died. The shock was profound. Yes, I have my writing, but the stories that I fashioned once were fairy tales, and they would not satisfy me now.

writer in real life that he, or she, realises the full impact of its meaning. When my husband died it was as though the sheltered cloudland that had enveloped me for years, peopled with images drawn from my imagination, suddenly dissolved, and I was face to face with a harsh and terrible reality. This sudden, apparently irredeemable wrench away from one's imaginative life was to find expression in the novel I wrote about Kilmarth.

The drawing room, or long room as I call it, where I spend much of the day.

Butterflies – the place abounds with them - flitting among the buddleia.

Kilmarth, today, has a slated eighteenth-century front, with twentieth-century additions on either side. The front garden is enclosed by walls and railings, giving a formal touch, and, although it was suggested I should take down the Victorian porch, I am glad I kept it; it has a delightful, old-fashioned air. Wild life abounds here as much as at Menabilly. Badgers scratch the earth beneath tumbled leaves, jackdaws roost in the taller trees, owls hoot by night, and as for butterflies, the place abounds with them – tortoiseshell, swallow-tail, admirals, flitting among the overgrown buddleia. And the long summer through swallows and martins build under the eaves.

Gradually I begin to 'grow' into the new house, taking something of its atmosphere into myself and giving something in return.

From an old man in the nearby village of Tywardreath I discover that the house dates back to the fourteenth century, and, from the County Record Office, that in 1327 one Roger Kylmerth owned it and that the foundations of his house are beneath me now.

So it was that I found the storyline for *The House on the Strand*. It would be set both in the present and the past. Like Peter Ibbetson, the hero Dick Young would travel back in time, in this case the fourteenth-century world of Roger Kylmerth. And he would do this not by dreaming true but by means of a drug prepared by his friend – a professor of biophysics named Magnus Lane – in the laboratory full of curious exhibits that I had found in the basement

The Roger Kylmerth who lived here in 1327 may have been different in character from the one I have written about in The House on the Strand, *but the foundations of his home are beneath me now. This is the basement where Professor Singer (Magnus Lane) had his laboratory and produced the time drug.*

of Kilmarth, close to the foundations of Kylmerth's house.

When I sit down to write a novel I am not consciously trying to please the reading public, but I did wonder, as I finished *The House on the Strand*, whether people would be put off when they heard it was about a time drug. Fortunately they weren't, and if nothing else my use of the drug is a clue to the time of its writing. The late '60s was the era of LSD. Aspects of Dick's altered state of consciousness are certainly similar to the LSD experience, and as a result people have asked me whether I tried LSD before writing the novel. The answer is that I did not. The nearest I ever came to experimenting with drugs was when I was writing *The Life of Branwell Brontë*. I remember I was able to obtain a prescription of laudanum, a tiny bottle, so that I could see exactly what Branwell felt like. But when I was ready, I lost my nerve and poured it down the sink.

Here, Dick describes his first experience of the drug.

The first thing I noticed was the clarity of the air, and then the sharp green colour of the land. There was no softness anywhere. The distant hills did not blend into the sky but stood out like rocks, so close that I could almost touch them, their proximity giving me that shock of surprise and wonder which a child feels looking for the first time through a telescope. Nearer to me, too, each object had the same hard quality, the very grass turning to single blades, springing from a younger, harsher soil than the soil I knew.

I had expected – if I expected anything – a transformation of another kind: a tranquil sense of well-being, the blurred intoxication of a dream, with

Polmear Hill: 'I was walking downhill towards the sea, across the fields of sharp-edged silver grass.'

Top: *Par beach – 'There was nothing left but grass and scrub, and the high distant hills that seemed so near.'*

Right: *The almshouses at the base of Polmear Hill. In 1327, 'the sea swept inland here, forming a creek that cut to the east, into the valley.'*

everything about me misty, ill-defined; not this tremendous impact, a reality more vivid than anything hitherto experienced, sleeping or awake. Now every impression was heightened, every part of me singularly aware: eyesight, hearing, sense of smell, all had been in some way sharpened.

All but the sense of touch: I could not feel the ground beneath my feet. Magnus had warned me of this. He had told me, 'You won't be aware of your body coming into contact with inanimate objects. You will walk, stand, sit, brush against them, but will feel nothing. Don't worry. The very fact that you can move without sensation is half the wonder.'

This, of course, I had taken as a joke, one of the many bribes to goad me to experiment. Now he was proved right. I started to go forward, and the sensation was exhilarating, for I seemed to move without effort, feeling no contact with the ground.

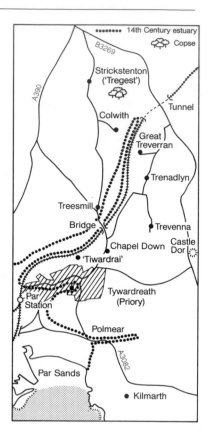

I was walking downhill towards the sea, across those fields of sharp-edged silver grass that glistened under the sun, for the sky – dull, a moment ago, to my ordinary eyes – was now cloudless, a blazing ecstatic blue. I remembered that the tide had been out, the stretches of flat sand exposed, the row of bathing-huts, lined like dentures in an open mouth, forming a solid background to the golden expanse. Now they had gone, and with them the rows of houses fronting the road, the docks, all of Par – chimneys, rooftops, buildings – and the sprawling tentacles of St Austell enveloping the countryside beyond the bay. There was nothing left but grass and scrub, and the high distant hills that seemed so near; while before me the sea rolled into the bay, covering the whole stretch of sand as if a tidal wave had swept over the land, swallowing it in one rapacious draught. To the north-west, the cliffs came down to meet the sea, which, narrowing gradually, formed a wide estuary, the waters sweeping inward, following the curve of the land and so vanishing out of sight.

When I came to the edge of the cliff and looked beneath me, where the road should be, the inn, the café, the almshouses at the base of Polmear hill, I realised that the sea swept inland here as well, forming a creek that cut to the east, into the valley. Road and houses had gone, leaving only a dip between the land which rose on either side of the creek. Here the channel ran narrowly between banks of mud and sand, so that at low tide the water would surely seep away, leaving a marshy track that could be forded, if not on foot, at least by a horseman. I descended the hill and stood beside the creek, trying to pinpoint in my mind the exact course of the road I knew, but already the old sense of orientation had gone: there was nothing to serve as guide except the ground itself, the valley and the hills.

The waters of the narrow channel rippled swift and blue over the sand, leaving on either side a frothy scum. Bubbles formed, expanded and vanished, and all the ordinary timeless waste came drifting with the tide, tresses of dark seaweed, feathers, twigs, the aftermath of some autumnal gale. I knew, in my own time, it was high summer, however dull and overcast the day, but all about me now was the clear light of approaching winter, surely an early afternoon when the bright sun, already flaming in the west, would turn the sky dark crimson before the night clouds came.

The first live things swam into vision, gulls following the tide, small waders skimming the surface of the stream, while high on the opposite hill, sharply defined against the skyline, a team of oxen ploughed their steady course. I closed my eyes, then opened them again. The team had vanished behind the rise of the field they worked, but the cloud of gulls, screaming in their wake, told me they had been a living presence, no figment of a dream.

I drank deep of the cold air, filling my lungs. Just to breathe was a joy never yet experienced for its own sake, having some quality of magic that I had not sensed before. Impossible to analyse thought, impossible to let my reason play on what I saw: in this new world of perception and delight there was nothing but intensity of feeling to serve as guide.

I might have stood for ever, entranced, content to hover between earth and sky, remote from any life I knew or cared to know; but then I turned my head and saw that I was not alone. The hoofs had made no sound – the pony must have travelled as I had done, across the fields – and now that it trod upon the shingle the clink of stone against metal came to my ears with a sudden shock, and I could smell the warm horse-flesh, sweaty and strong.

Instinct made me back away, startled, for the rider came straight towards me, unconscious of my presence.

Dick, a publisher, has been enticed to Kilmarth by the promise of long lazy days in the sun. He is there alone; Magnus is in London; Vita, Dick's American wife, is due to join him in a week or so, with her two boys – sons from an earlier marriage. The 'condition' of Dick's summer tenure is to act as guinea pig for Magnus's drug. His first 'trip' takes him to Tywardreath church, where he is led by his companion in time – the rider, who is in fact Roger Kylmerth – through the doors of a priory occupied by a

The church at Tywardreath: 'I got out of the car, opened the iron gates into the churchyard and stood in the church porch.'

dissolute order of French monks attached to the Benedictine Abbey of St Sergius and Bacchus in Angers. The year is 1328.

The rider turned left, dismounted before the walled enclosure, flung his reins over a staple in the ground, and entered through a broad, brass-studded doorway. Above the arch there was a carving showing the robed figure of a saint, holding in his right hand the cross of St Andrew. My Catholic training, long forgotten, even mocked, made me cross myself before that door, and as I did so a bell sounded from within, striking so profound a chord in my memory that I hesitated before entering, dreading the old power that might turn me back into the childhood mould.

I need not have worried. The scene that met my eyes was not that of orderly paths and quadrangles, quiet cloisters, the odour of sanctity, the silence born of prayer. The gate opened upon a muddied yard, round which two men were chasing a frightened boy, flicking at his bare thighs with flails. Both, from their dress and tonsure, were monks, and the boy a novice, his skirt secured above his waist to make their sport more piquant.

The horseman watched the pantomime unmoved, but when the boy at last fell, his habit about his ears, his skinny limbs and bare backside exposed, he called, 'Don't bleed him yet. The Prior likes sucking-pig served without sauce. The garnish will come later when the piglet turns tough.' Meanwhile the bell for prayer continued, without effect upon the sportsmen in the yard.

Dazzled by the effect of the drug Dick decides to repeat the experience the following day, and drives back to Tywardreath church in his car.

I drove slowly up the drive, turned left out of the lane to the main road, and went down Polmear hill, pausing when I reached the bottom to survey the scene. Here, where the almshouses and the inn stood now, had been yesterday's ford. The lie of the land had not altered, despite the modern road, but the valley where the tide had swept inward was now marsh. I took the lane to Tywardreath, thinking, with some misgiving, that if I had in fact taken this same route yesterday, under the influence of the drug, I could have been knocked down by a passing car without hearing it.

I drove down the steep, narrow lane to the village and parked the car a little above the church. There was still a light rain falling, and nobody was about. A van drove up the main Par road and disappeared. A woman came out of the grocer's shop and walked uphill in the same direction. No one else appeared. I got out of the car, opened the iron gates into the churchyard, and stood in the church porch to shelter from the rain. The churchyard itself sloped away in a southerly direction until it terminated at the boundary wall, and beneath it were farm-buildings. Yesterday, in that other world, there were no buildings, only the blue waters of a creek filling the valley with the incoming tide, and the Priory buildings had coverd the space the churchyard held today.

I knew the lie of the land better now. If the drug took effect I could leave the car where it was and walk home. There was no one around. Then, like a diver taking a plunge into some arctic pool, I took the flask and swallowed

'Like a diver taking a plunge into some arctic pool, I took the flask and swallowed the contents.'

'Yesterday, in that other world, there were only the blue waters of a creek filling the valley with the incoming tide, and the Priory buildings had covered the space the churchyard held today.'

the contents. The instant I had done so panic seized me. This second dose might have a quite different effect. Make me sleep for hours. Should I stay where I was, or should I be better off in the car? The church porch gave me claustrophobia, so I went out and sat down on one of the tombstones, not far from the pathway but out of sight of the road. If I stayed quite still, without moving, perhaps nothing would happen. I began to pray, 'Don't let anything happen. Don't let the drug have any effect.'

I went on sitting for about five minutes, too apprehensive about the possible effects of the drug to mind the rain. Then I heard the church clock strike three, and glanced down at my watch to check the time. It was a few minutes slow, so I altered it, and almost immediately I heard shouting from the village, or cheering, perhaps – a curious mélange of the two – and a creaking sound like wheels. Oh God, what now, I thought, a travelling circus about to descend the village street? I shall have to move the car. I got up and started to walk along the path to the churchyard gate. I never arrived, because the gate had gone, and I was looking through a rounded window set in a stone wall, the window facing a cobbled quadrangle bounded by shingle paths.

There gathered together for an imminent visit by Bishop Grandisson of Exeter Cathedral (at that time the episcopal See took in both Cornwall and Devon), are monks and local dignitaries – Lord of the Manor Henry de Champernoune, his wife Joanna (to whom Roger is steward), her brother Sir Otto Bodrugan, Sir John Carminowe, keeper of the King's forests and parks in Cornwall, his brother Sir Oliver Carminowe and Sir Oliver's wife, the lovely Isolda.

At one point Dick suspects some sort of thought transference from Magnus Lane, closeted in his university cell in London. But time and again he is able to verify his experiences in the history books. He learns from the parish priest that there was a priory in the present churchyard of Tywardreath (you can see the tombstone of the last prior in the north transept of the church). Bishop Grandisson, Henry and Joanna de Champernoune, the Bodrugans from their estate across the bay, the Carminowes, Isolda, all are verified. The manor house, home of the Champernounes, is

The tombstone to the last Prior, who had been buried before the altar in 1538.

In search of Tiwardrai, the House on the Strand, Dick walks to Treesmill: 'The narrow road ran steeply to a valley, and before the final descent sloped sharply to a humped-backed bridge.'

The 'sluggish stream' at the base of the hill, in 1327 a deep estuary leading up beyond Colwith.

mentioned in Domesday though no trace of the building remains today. Dick discovers that its name, Tiwardrai, means House on the Strand, and he decides to find it.

I drove up through Tywardreath and took the left-hand fork to Treesmill. The narrow road, with fields on either side of it, ran steeply to a valley, and before the final descent sloped sharply to a humped-backed bridge beneath which the main railway line ran between Par and Plymouth. I braked by the bridge and heard the hoot of the diesel express as it emerged from the tunnel out of sight to my right, and in a few moments the train itself came rattling down the line, passed under the bridge, and curved its way through the valley down to Par. Memories of undergraduate days came back to me. Magnus and I had always travelled down by train, and directly the train came out of the tunnel between Lostwithiel and Par we used to reach for our suitcases. I had been aware, then, of steep fields to the left of the carriage window and a valley to the right, full of reeds and stumpy willows, and suddenly the train would be at the station, the large black board with the white lettering announcing 'Par Change For Newquay', and we should have arrived.

Now, watching the express disappear round the bend in the valley, I

The old mill-house, Treesmill.

observed the terrain from another angle, and realized how the coming of the railway over a hundred years ago must have altered the sloping fields, the line literally dug out of the hillside. There had been other disturbers of the peace besides the railway. Quarries had scarred the opposite side of the valley on the high ground where the tin and copper mines had flourished a century ago – I remembered Commander Lane telling us once at dinner how hundreds of men had been employed in the mines in Victorian days, and when the slump came, chimneys and engine-houses were left to crumble into decay, the miners emigrating, or seeking work in the newer industry of china clay.

This afternoon, the train out of sight and the rattle spent, all was quiet once again, and nothing moved in the valley except a few cows grazing in the swampy meadow at the base of the hill. I let the car descend gently to the end of the road before it rose sharply again to climb the opposite hill out of the valley. A sluggish stream ran through the meadow where the cows were grazing, spanned by a low bridge, and above the stream, to the right of the road, were old farm-buildings. I lowered the window of the car and looked about me. A dog ran from the farm, barking, followed by a man carrying a pail. I leant out of the window and asked him if this was Treesmill.

'Yes,' he said. 'If you continue straight on you'll come to the main road from Lostwithiel to St Blazey.'

'In point of fact,' I answered, 'I was looking for the mill itself.'

'Nothing left of it,' he said. 'This building here was the old mill-house, and all that's left of the stream is what you see. The main stream was diverted many years ago, before my time. They tell me that before they built this bridge there was a ford here. The stream ran right across this road, and most of the valley was under water.'

'Yes,' I said, 'yes, that's very possible.'

He pointed to a cottage the other side of the bridge. 'That used to be a pub in old days,' he said, 'when they were working the mines up at Lanescot and Carrogett. It would be full of miners on a Saturday night, so they tell me. Not many people alive who know much about the old days now.'

'Do you know,' I asked him, 'if there is any farmhouse here in the valley that might have been a manor-house in days gone by?'

He considered a moment before replying. 'Well,' he said, 'there's Trevenna up back behind us, on the Stonybridge road, but I've never heard it was old, and Trenadlyn beyond that, and of course Treverran up the valley nearer the railway tunnel. That's an old house all right, fine old place, built hundreds of years ago.'

'How long ago?' I inquired, interest rising.

He considered again. 'There was a piece about Treverran in the paper once,' he said. 'Some gentleman from Oxford went to look at it. I believe it was 1705 they said it was built.'

My interest ebbed. Queen Anne houses, tin and copper mines, the pub across the road, all these were centuries later than my time. I felt as an archaeologist must feel who discovers a late Roman villa instead of a Bronze Age camp.

'Well, thanks very much,' I said, 'good day to you,' and turned the car and drove back up the hill. . .

I had reached the summit of the hill, and beyond the lay-by the road curved down to Tywardreath. Below a house called Chapel Down, a gate led into a field, and I climbed over it, circuiting the field and keeping close to the hedge until the sloping ground hid me from sight.

I lit a cigarette and surveyed the scene . . . Treesmill farm away to my right, the other farms beyond, all sheltered from prevailing wind and weather, immediately below me the railway, and beyond it the strange sweep of the valley, no pattern of fields, nothing but a tapestry of willow, birch and alder. A paradise, surely, for birds in spring, and a good place for boys to hide from the parental eye – but boys never went bird's-nesting nowadays, at least my stepsons didn't.

I sat down against the hedge to finish my cigarette, and as I did so became aware of the flask in my breast pocket. I took it out and looked at it. It was a handy size, and I wondered if it had belonged to Magnus's father; it would have been just right for a nip of rum in his sailing days, when the breeze freshened. If only Vita had disliked flying and had chosen to come by sea it would have given me several more days . . . A rattle beneath me made me look down to the valley. A solitary diesel engine was coming up the line, going hell for leather without its load of carriages, and I watched it worm its way, like a fat, swift-moving slug, above the willows and the birches, pass under the bridge over Treesmill, and disappear finally into the gaping jaws of the tunnel a mile distant. I unscrewed the flask and downed its contents.

All right, I told myself, so what? I'm bloody-minded. And Vita's still in mid-Atlantic. I closed my eyes.

This time, sitting motionless with my back against the hedge and my eyes shut, I would try to pinpoint the moment of transition. On the previous occasions I had been walking, the first time across fields, the second up the churchyard path, when the vision altered. Now it would surely happen otherwise, because I was concentrating on the moment of impact. The sense of well-being would come, like a burden being lifted, and with it the sensation of lightness as feeling went from my body. No panic today, and no dismal falling rain. It was even warm, and the sun must be breaking through the clouds – I could sense the brightness through my closed eyelids. I took a last pull at the fag-end of my cigarette and let it drop.

If this drowsy content lasted much longer I might even fall asleep. Even the birds were rejoicing in the burst of sunshine; I could hear the blackbird singing in the hedge somewhere behind me, and more delightfully still a cuckoo called from the valley, distant at first, then near at hand. I listened to the call, a favourite sound, connected in my mind with every sort of carefree boyhood ramble thirty years ago. There, he called again, immediately overhead.

I opened my eyes and watched him wing his strange, unsteady flight across the sky, and as he did so I remembered that it was late July. The cuckoo's brief English summer ceased in June, along with the blackbird's song, and the primroses that were blooming in the bank beside me would have withered by mid-May. This warmth and brightness belonged to another world, an earlier spring. It had happened, despite concentration, in a moment of time that had not registered in my brain. All the sharp green colour of that first day was spread about me on the sloping hill below, and the valley with its tapestry of birch and willow lay submerged beneath a sheet of water, part of a great winding estuary that cut into the land, bordered by sandbanks where the water shallowed. I stood up, and saw how the river narrowed to mingle with the tumbling mill-stream below Treesmill, the farmhouse altered in shape, narrow, thatched, the hills opposite thickly forested with oak, the foliage young and tender because of spring.

Immediately beneath me, where the field had shelved precipitously to the railway cutting, the ground took on a gentler slope, in the midst of which a broad track ran to the estuary, the track terminating in a quay beside which boats were anchored, the channel there being deep, forming a natural pool. A larger vessel was moored in mid-stream, her sail partly stowed. I could hear the voices of the men aboard her singing, and as I watched a smaller boat alongside pushed off to ferry someone ashore, and the voices were suddenly hushed, as the passenger in the small boat lifted his hand for silence. Now I looked around me, and the hedge had gone, the hill behind me was thickly wooded like the hills opposite, and to my left, where there had been scrub and gorse, a long stone wall encircled a dwelling-house; I could see the rooftop above the surrounding trees. The path from the quay led straight uphill to the house.

The field, opposite Chapel Down, which 'shelved precipitously to the railway cutting' where Dick takes his third 'trip' and discovers the House on the Strand.

I drew nearer, watching the man below descend from the boat at the quay, then proceed to climb the road towards me. As he did so the cuckoo called again, flying overhead, and the man looked up to watch it, pausing for breath as he climbed, his action so ordinary, so natural, that it endeared him to me for no reason except that he lived, and I was a ghost in time.

Scientists are not prepared to acknowledge that a sixth sense capable of looking back into the past or forward to the future exists, or, when they do, they (like Magnus Lane) explain it in material terms, as a memory storehouse, connected to the brain. Late in the novel, in a letter to Dick Young, Professor Lane explains how the drug works to tap our 'ancestral memory'.

'Dear Dick,' I read, 'I'm writing this in the train, and it will probably be illegible. If I find a post-box handy on Exeter station I'll drop it in. There is probably no need to write at all, and by the time you receive it on Saturday morning we shall have had, I trust, an uproarious evening together with many more to come, but I write as a safety-measure, in case I pass out in the carriage from sheer exuberance of spirits. My findings to date are pretty conclusive that we are on to something of prime importance regarding the brain. Briefly, and in layman's language, the chemistry within the brain cells concerned with memory, everything we have done from infancy onwards, is reproducible, returnable, for want of a better term, in these same cells, the exact contents of which depends upon our hereditary make-up, the legacy of parents, grandparents, remoter ancestors back to primeval times. The fact that I am a genius and you are a lay-about depends solely upon the messages transmitted to us from these cells and then distributed through the various other cells and throughout our body, but, our various characteristics apart, the particular cells I have been working upon – which I will call the memory-box – store not only our own memories but habits of the earlier brain pattern we inherit. These habits, if released to consciousness, would enable us to see, hear, become cognoscent of things that happened in the past, not because any particular ancestor witnessed any particular scene, but because with the use of a medium – in this case a drug – the inherited, older brain pattern takes over and becomes dominant. The implications from a historian's point of view don't concern me, but, biologically, the potential uses of the hitherto untapped ancestral brain are of enormous interest, and open immeasurable possibilities. . .

Magnus'

I find the science of genetics, of which I knew little in my youth, exciting, even exhilarating. The colour of our eyes, our skin, the shape of our hands, the depth of our emotions, the bump of humour or lack of it, the small talents we may put to good account, even the ill-health that suddenly in later life descends without apparent reason – these are the things that make us what we are. As an individual living here and now I am only too well aware that I possess feelings, emotions, a mind and body bequeathed to me by people long since dead who have made me what I am. Generations of French craftsmen of the tight-knit glass-blowing fraternity, provincial, clannish, have handed onto me a strong family sense, a wary suspicion of all who are not 'us'.

There is no cell in our bodies that has not been transmitted to us by our ancestors, and the very blood group may predispose us to the disease that finally kills. We are all of us chemical particles, inherited not only from our parents but from a million ancestors. Our past is virtually limitless.

For this reason alone none of us is isolated in time, a mere expression of the present. In a very real sense, 'yesterday is within us'. We are part of what we were once and of what we are yet to become in successive generations. But for me the novel would be more than an exploration of the logical possibilities of genetic theory. Dick's travels back into the past are mine, the writer's. We have walked together, Dick and I, about that other world 'with a dreamer's freedom but with a waking man's perception'. I share with him the empathy that he feels with the lives of his fourteenth-century characters because it is so similar to how I felt when writing about the people who had built and sailed *Jane Slade*, or the people who had lived and died once at Menabilly. 'Intense involvement but intense compassion too. Yes, that was the word, compassion. And I had no way of explaining my sense of participation in all they did, unless it was that stepping backwards out of my time to theirs, I felt them vulnerable, and more certainly doomed to die than I was myself, knowing indeed, that they had been dust for more than six centuries.'

Like the writer of his story, Dick thrills to the excavating of the past. 'Roger [Kylmerth] had been no faded snapshot in time's album; and even now, in this fourth dimension into which I had stumbled, he lived and moved, ate and slept, beneath me in his house, Kylmerth, enacting his living Now which ran side by side with my immediate Present. . . There was no past, no present, no future. Everything living is part of the whole. We are all bound, one to the other, through time and eternity, and, our senses once opened, as mine have been opened by the drug, to a new understanding of his world and mine, fusion would take place, there would be no separation, there would be no death. . . This would be the ultimate meaning of the experiment, surely, that by moving about in time death was destroyed. This was what Magnus so far had not understood. To him, the drug released the complex brew within the brain that served up the savoured past. To me, it proved that the past was living still, that we are all participants, all witnesses. I was Roger, I was Bodrugan, I was Cain; and in being so was more truly myself.'

Dick becomes obsessed with the motivations and injustices of the people and plots he uncovers in the other world, even though none of its inhabitants can sense his presence. He becomes resentful of the time he must spend in the mundane 'un-real' world of his American wife Vita, who has arrived at Kilmarth more concerned

The obsession to find Tregest, the house of the beautiful Isolda Carminowe, leads to Magnus Lane's death when the 20th Century, in the form of a passing freight train, intrudes upon his imaginary world.

The quest for Isolda and the 14th-century Tregest absorbs Magnus and Dick, as completely as the imaginary characters and plots absorb me when I sit in front of my typewriter and a story unfolds.

Read the novel, then follow Dick out of Treesmill, taking the turning to Colwith. You'll find the 'small water-splash at the bottom of the hill' where Dick parks his car before his seventh 'trip'.

Left: *Dick walks upstream 'knowing by instinct that if I kept the river on my left I must be moving north'. He comes upon a copse of trees from which some half-dozen dogs, yelping and crying, splash their way into the water in chase of an otter.*

Dogs and men drive the hunted otter into the gulley that feeds the stream, 'and in a moment they were upon him, the dogs crying, the men thrashing with their sticks'. One of the men is Oliver Carminowe who leads Dick to Isolda's house on the hillside beyond the copse, at Strickstenton.

Henceforth Dick opts to live in his imaginary world. When it dissolves as surely it must, he too comes face to face with a harsh and terrible reality.

about today than the possibilities of yesterday.

Meanwhile Magnus, enthused by Dick's telephone reports of his experiences, travels down to Cornwall by train to help him in his quest for the elusive last piece of a jigsaw that will complete the reality of the fourteenth-century world – the whereabouts of Isolda Carminowe's house, Tregest. Following a hunch, Magnus alights at Par station and takes a dose of his drug, making his way along the Stonybridge lane above Trecsmill past Trenadlyn Farm. But before he reaches the main road he turns off into a field they call Higher Gum, and crosses it in the direction of the railway line. There, in a world where there exist no lines, no signals, no warning hoots sounding in the air, he is struck and killed by a passing train.

Appalled by the tragedy but yet more determined to pursue his quest, Dick finds his Tregest and ensconsed in his 14th-century world, follows Isolda and Roger back to Kylmerth. There, Dick makes his fatal mistake, personally intervening in a jealous attempt by Joanna de Champernoune to destroy the future happiness of Isolda, banishing her from her retreat at Kylmerth.

Joanna stared towards me, her eyes opening wide, and I did not care what happened afterwards, I wanted to put my hands round her throat and choke her before she vanished, like the others, out of sight. I crossed the room and stood beside her, and she did not fade. She began to scream, as I shook her backwards and forwards, my hands round her plump, white neck.

'Damn you,' I shouted, 'damn you. . .damn you. . .' and the screaming was all around me, and above as well. I loosened my grip and looked up, and the boys were crouching there on the landing at the top of the back stairs, and Vita had fallen against the banister beside me, and was staring at me, white-faced, terrified, her hands to her throat . . .

As past and present collide, Dick falls victim to his illusions, as anyone must who seeks to attach undue significance to perceptions that can be no more (nor less) than hieroglyphics – the words of a novelist on a page.

The view from the bedroom at Kilmarth is the best I have ever known. The ilex trees have a magic quality, outlined against the sky.

In truth, time defines our human existence. Only our mortality offers us the promise of our beliefs and intuitions. And perhaps that is the great irony of the death we all so fear.

> *Last night the other world came much too near,*
> *And with it fear.*
> *I heard their voices whisper me from sleep,*
> *And could not keep*
> *My mind upon the dream, for still they came,*
> *Calling my name,*
> *The loathly keepers of the netherland*
> *I understand.*
> *My frozen brain rejects the pulsing beat;*
> *My willing feet,*
> *Cloven like theirs, too swiftly recognise*
> *Without surprise.*
> *The horn that echoes from the further hill,*
> *Discordant, shrill,*
> *Has such a leaping urgency of song,*
> *Too loud, too long,*
> *That prayer is stifled like a single note*
> *In the parched throat.*
> *How fierce the flame! How beautiful and bright*
> *The inner light*
> *Of that great world which lives within our own,*
> *Remote, alone.*
> *Let me not see too soon, let me not know,*
> *And so forgo*
> *All that I cling to here, the safety side*
> *Where I would bide.*
> *Old Evil, loose my chains and let me rest*
> *Where I am best,*
> *Here in the muted shade of my own dust.*
> *But if I must*
> *Go wandering in Time and seek the source*
> *Of my life force,*
> *Lend me your sable wings, that as I fall*
> *Beyond recall,*
> *The sober stars may tumble in my wake,*
> *For Jesus' sake.*

ANOTHER WORLD

EPILOGUE

As I approach my eighty-third year I still love walking on my own; it's become a sort of ritual. I go out over the cliffs and down to the beach where I used to swim, and then back again. It's not lonely, it's just that I've always liked being on my own. If I had to choose something to do, I think I'd be a shepherd on the mountains in Crete, standing, leaning upon a staff and pottering with the sheep.

I have an awful feeling that the spirit of Cornwall is changing, the quietude, the solitude of it all. In the final chapter of *Vanishing Cornwall*, which I wrote twenty-two years ago now, I ask the question, 'What does the future hold for Cornwall?' Will it indeed become the playground of all England,

I still love walking. I go out over the cliffs and down to the beach where I used to swim, and then back again. If I had to choose something to do, I think I'd be a shepherd on the mountains in Crete, standing, leaning upon a staff and pottering with the sheep.

chalets and holiday-camps set close to every head-land, despite the efforts of the county planning authorities and the National Trust to preserve the coast?

I provided a sort of answer in my last novel *Rule Britannia*. At that time, in the early seventies, there was a terrific lot going on in Northern Ireland, people resenting the army, and I thought I wonder how Cornwall would do if suddenly friendly soldiers, like the Americans, landed. Who would resist and who collaborate? So, in the novel, Cornwall is invaded not by tourists but by the American army. A new USUK alliance has been formed in the wake of economic disaster, and the Americans have a clear idea about where the remedy lies.

Plans for Great Britain herself would take some little time to formulate. It must be recognised that her heyday as a great industrial nation had now ended, but a new future lay ahead for her as the historical and cultural centre of the English-speaking peoples. Just as some years previously people on holiday had gone in their thousands to the Costa Brava in Spain for sea and sunshine, so now tourists would flock in their millions to explore the country that had given birth to Shakespeare, Milton, Lord Byron. . .

'Don't you see,' said Martha Hubbard, 'that what you have to sell here in the UK is not sunshine or bathing beaches, but historical background. Why, the whole of the west coast from north Wales down to Cornwall here can be developed as one vast leisure-land. With the good Welsh folk dressed in their costumes, tall hats and cloaks, serving potato-cakes to the tourists from the States, they wouldn't be talking any more of unemployment. The same in Cornwall. Now, we in the States don't need to purchase your clay, but construct a miniature Switzer-land out of your white mountains and train your unemployed as ski instructors and sleigh-drivers. . .'

It was Fortress Cornwall a decade before the Falklands, but I fear that the plans for exploiting our great heritage may have been just as prophetic.

A lot of people who think of me as a recluse, shut away in a remote house on the cliffs in Cornwall, identify me with Mad in *Rule Britannia*. She's the rather left-wing, eccentric actress who dresses in an outfit reminiscent of 'the uniform worn by the late lamented Mao Tse-tung', lives in a house like mine overlooking the bay, and has no intention of letting the Americans have their way.

I don't mind that, if the same people also attribute something of Mad's spirit of resistance to me. I'm sure my grandchildren would. While the story was brewing the young Browning boys spent their summer holidays here at Kilmarth, rushing about the woods, playing with their Action Men. As an old girl, past her prime, I could hardly join in their war games. But I was the first to encourage 'An Attack' on the ruined cottage in the shrubbery! And would secretly watch from a window whilst these daily battles raged in the summer sun.

A lot of myself did indeed go into the character of Mad, and sometimes it's very easy to think of Kilmarth as an outpost, a last frontier. And how appropriate, for shortly before moving here I discovered that the word 'Kilmarth' in Cornish means 'Retreat of Mark'. Perhaps this site was also the last outpost of the aged Cornish king (King Mark of the Tristan legend) who, with passion spent and jealousy forgotten, came, like me, to rest and look out in peace across the sea.

INDEX

Acknowledgements

Quotations from the following books by Daphne du Maurier by kind permission of
Victor Gollancz Limited, London, and Doubleday, Inc, New York:

The Loving Spirit	Vanishing Cornwall
Jamaica Inn	The House on the Strand
Rebecca	Rule Britannia
Frenchman's Creek	Growing Pains
The King's General	The Rebecca Notebook
My Cousin Rachel	The Birds
Castle Dor	

Photographs by Nick Wright, Piers Dudgeon, Christian Browning, The National Maritime Museum, Redruth Library, Tom Blau (Camera Press), Life Magazine, Frank Gibson, Bruce Coleman Ltd

Line maps by Rob Shone

With special thanks to Christian Browning for making available family archives and facilitating the producing of this book at every turn.